Two paths

Akash and Saroja. Saroja and Akash. The names were nearly synonymous. They grew up together. They were born one month apart. First came into the world, Saroja. Akash followed exactly one month later. They were like twins or more than twins—they were inseparable. They were the best of friends in the world. Their mothers were also friends, very good friends. They had their houses side by side in the bustling metropolis of Mumbai.

Saroja and Akash had identical upbringings in modern Mumbai. Akash went to America to pursue his dreams. Saroja stayed back. Their paths diverged and so did their lives. They kept in touch through letters. They wrote to each other the minutest details of their lives. Even though they didn't meet each other after they had parted, each knew exactly what was happening in the other's life. Sometimes there were lulls because of a major event in one or the other's life, but they wrote their hearts out till the end.

Now, we get to read the letters they had penned exclusively for the other's eyes. We will see exactly what was happening in their lives, not only from the perspective of what others around them could see, but what they themselves saw.

Table of Contents:

Chapter I. Hello, America

Dear Saroja,

I landed in Seattle. It was evening time. You can't possibly fathom my excitement as I was disembarking from the airplane. I had wondered if the land in America would look different from the land in our mother India. As I got out of the plane, the first thing I looked at was the moon. The pleasant white light had engulfed the landmass. What struck me was, the moon looked exactly the same. I couldn't help but wonder if it was the same moon you and I had looked at for hours on end in our childhoods. I was overjoyed. I wanted to savor the moment. I knew that experience was irreplicable because it's only once that you can land on the American soil for the first time.

When I took a taxi to my boarding, to my surprise the cab driver was a Punjabi. I couldn't tell that though. He was tall, and may be a bit dark skinned (like me). But, he struck a conversation with me, which I initially found weird. We hardly utter a word to our cab and auto-rickshaw drivers in India. I was looking out the window taking in the views of what appeared to me, pine trees. The vegetation here is quite different. It's not our Banyan trees, and middle height trees that we are used to seeing. The trees here are quite tall, twice or thrice the height of trees that you and I were used to seeing. I had only read about these trees in geography books. I reckon these trees are evergreen trees. The leaves are like Christmas tree leaves. By the bye, I could see snow capped mountains in the distance. Anyway, back to the cab driver. He probably saw me curiously looking out the window with awe. So, the first question he asked me was, "First time in America?" I was startled how he knew. I didn't ask. I only said, yes. Then, he started telling me he was from Punjab. Another thing I thought he thought about me was, I was there for the long haul because he started telling me to not trust strangers all that much, and not leave my luggage in the custody of people I didn't know, like I guess, we sometimes do in India. He said, "When you come back, you may not find your luggage, and the person may just say 'Sorry, I don't know', and vanish." We reached our hotel. It was called "Blue Star". I got out of the taxi, paid the driver a $50 bill and asked him to keep the change. He looked happy. I had read before coming here that tipping is a norm in America. I made it a point to not flunk on that point right off the bat.

I was walking into the entrance and a lady (I should say quite a stout one at that) looked at me and said "Hi". I was quite shocked. There was no chance I could have met her in India. I timidly said, hi too. I opened the front door and a beautiful girl maybe my age was peeking in from the inside. She asked, "Can I help you?" I said, "Yes". I needed help desperately. After explaining the matter, she told me my room number, handed me the keys and bid me goodbye. She gave me vague directions on how to get there. The hotel rooms here were not stacked one top of the other but were laid out in a sprawling campus. I had a desire to ask her to show me the room, but I thought that that may be inappropriate because I was a single man asking a beautiful girl to lead me to my room. She was friendly throughout (all business folks seem friendly here). I started lugging my luggage in search of my reserved room. After some fumbling about, I did reach it. Another thing I noticed was that the property was not ringed by a compound wall. Instead, there were short shrubs guarding it, which I found quite distinct from tall compound walls we erect around pretty much everything in India. The room that I entered was not just a room. It was the size of an apartment. The weather was gloomy. It was cloudy but was not very cold. This was the month of April. Later I found out that this is Spring time in Seattle. I was lucky to have landed here when mother Earth was blossoming. I freshened up and ate something that I had brought with me. I wanted to charge my phone. I tried to find an electric socket but no, there was none. Well, there were quite a few, what appeared to be electric sockets. But, they couldn't be because I couldn't plug in my charger. The size of the holes was quite different. It was already 6 o'clock in the evening. The front office must have closed and the pretty lady must have disappeared, I reckoned. There was a contact number listed on one of the information sheets that they had left for me in the room. I rang up the number and explained the problem. The lady on the other end was incredulous. She thought I was loony to suggest that there were no electric sockets. She probably even thought I was playing a prank on her. After some back and forth, she told me she would send in somebody to help me out the next day. I said, "OK", and hung up the phone. By this time, I was feeling miserable and lonely. There was not a soul to be seen in the vicinity. Maybe there were people but all of them must have been indoors. There was still some light, so I thought I would take a stroll and look around. I put on my jacket, took my bulky camera and headed out. The road abutting the property was quite large. I was mesmerized. It was like a straight out of a movie scene. There were big jeeps, and big cars plying on the road. Most of the time, topless. The cars I mean. Often only two people, a couple most of the time I believe, would be sitting in the front seats expressionless and zoom past. The traffic was orderly. I stopped at a traffic signal waiting to cross. The lights would turn green, red, yellow everywhere but my "walk sign" would never come on. I was puzzled. I thought this was heaping injury upon injury. I was already on the verge of crying because of the loneliness that had engulfed me already and then I wasn't even allowed to walk! After I stood there nearly in tears for five minutes, a man walked to where I was standing and pushed a button on the light pole. In a minute, the walk sign came on. Ah, that was the trick. You had to push the walk sign request button and it would let you walk. Who knew? I was glad I found a way to walk around now. When there was a walk sign on and only him and I were walking, a cavalcade of motorists stood twenty feet way respectfully waiting for us to pass and the light for them to turn green. Nobody honked, nobody rushed to kill me while I was slowly making my way across. I walked some four miles that day. Every time I had to cross a road I felt bad—for this solitary man, each time some ten cars had to wait quite a while. There was no other way. I did press the button when I had to.

When I reached Seattle it was a Saturday and my work was to start the next Monday. My colleague did come over the next day and helped me set up the kitchen and buy groceries. Before I forget, the electrical socket problem also got resolved: it was just that I needed an electric adapter. The appliances in India run on 240V power whereas here they run on 120V. Plus, the size of the pins in the socket is also different. Once I bought an adapter, it was smooth sailing. Work was work. The office didn't look all that different from what I was used to back in Mumbai. The colleagues here are more diverse though— white Americans, black Americans, Asians, Indians and others of many other ethnicities. But, in terms of interactions, it was not much different. I was feeling terribly lonely by this time. I had only colleagues to talk to about work and the rest of the time, I was on my own. So, I started exploring the area in the evenings and especially on weekends. I got a bus pass, would hop onto a public transport bus and go where I wanted to go. I should describe the bus system here for you a little. Mind you, I learned all about it just by observing. Sometimes I feel proud that I was able to infer what I was able to infer. First, when you are waiting at a bus stop and the bus arrives, the bus driver may not necessarily stop. For him/her to stop (the bus drivers can be women too), you have to press again some sort of a button that turns on a light at the end of a pole. That is an indication that you want to board the bus. Even before I had gotten on any bus, I saw from a distance that a guy was loading up his bike on the front portion of the bus where there were dedicated bicycle stands. I found it so cool. The buses are built to accommodate bicycles. Once you get on a bus, you need to follow a protocol to get off at your intended stop. You have to pull a string and that would ring a bell, and it lets the driver know that they have to stop the bus at the next bus stop. If you don't pull the bell string in time, the driver will go on. That is what happened to me. I was hoping the driver would stop at the bus stop but he didn't. So, I rushed to the front and in my panicky voice I asked him to stop. He was good-natured and stopped for me a couple of hundred meters away from where the designated bus stop was. But, seeing me and knowing I might have been taking my first bus ride, he patiently explained what I should do the next time I wanted to get off the bus.

I did something else that I am sure you will find interesting. I know you have been a fan of dancing all your life. You had been begging me to join the Garbha dances with you, but I never did. I always found dancing to the Bollywood tunes senseless. What I did was, I danced to European classical music instead! I enrolled in dance classes and opted for private lessons. Ah, you won't believe it. I loved every second of my time on the dance floor. Sometimes there were other "students", but oftentimes it was only the instructor and me. She is a gorgeous blonde. Her name is Elizabeth. She is teaching me Salsa, Waltz and a few other forms whose names I was hearing for the first time. The first class was last Sunday at 10 am. I reached there just five minutes before 10 am with my leisurely walk. The dance studio was closed. Just when I thought maybe they forgot that they had scheduled me, a car pulled up. Out walked who but Elizabeth. One minute before it struck 10, she opened the door to the dance studio and at 10, we were on the dance floor. I am mightily impressed by their punctuality. It's ingrained in their culture. It's just so natural to be on time here for everything. She gave me her hand and said, "The entire dance floor is ours." Truth be told, I was feeling quite shy. I just followed her instructions. Seeing my awkwardness, it fell upon her to ease the uneasy silence. She asked, "How was your Saturday?" I merely said, "It was OK." I now realize I should have asked her how her weekend was going too. I was in such a state of perplexity that I had become dumb. She volunteered that they had gone to a park the previous day, sat on the grass and that it was wonderful. I didn't ask her who "they" were. Maybe it was she and her boyfriend. I don't know. It appears that having a boyfriend or a girlfriend is compulsory in America. Wherever you go, you see only couples. In India, you would see mother-son, father-daughter, brother-sister duos and grandfather-grandsons too, walking down the street. Here, no. It's only couples. That is the only relation that seems to exist. So in that sense, I am feeling a bit left out. Since I am new, I am not feeling a need to find a girlfriend as yet. I wouldn't mind having a girlfriend in my life.

Speaking of which, I think I am smitten by a girl. She is petite and incredibly beautiful. I only fancy her. I haven't mustered the courage to even say hello to her. She works in my office cafeteria. She appears young. She could be college going too for all you know. Here, people work while they study. She was at the checkout counter yesterday while I was buying my lunch—a box of Sushi, and an apple. She just says hello (she doesn't expect a reply) and collects the money. She has been handing me back the change—in dimes and nickels. I am yet to completely familiarize myself to count the coins correctly. There are a total of four checkout counters. Every day is a struggle. A part of me says I should go to another counter where she isn't, but the other part of me says, what's the harm, no one is noticing and so I can safely go to hers. Yesterday I was standing in her queue and as it happened (it sinks my heart thinking about this), her line was longer. I was at the back of the line and a middle aged lady called me over to her lane on the other side. I said to myself, "Good heavens, I am outed today". Outed that I am head over heels with that girl. Why would I otherwise spend five minutes extra standing in her line? When I am eating lunch, I keep furtively glancing at her. I always dread if she would notice this. If she does, I don't know what explanation I would have to offer her as to why I keep looking up at her. More than the question of if she would accept my invitation for coffee, what troubles me all the time is this: if she has a boyfriend. I find it too silly to admit—it breaks my heart to think she does. Cell phones are becoming a rage in America. She does carry a modest looking one. What I have observed is, she doesn't take it out while she is working. After the attendance in the cafeteria has dwindled though, she grabs what she wants (I think the food is free for the cafeteria workers) and sits down to eat. She does take out her phone then. She sometimes smiles to herself looking at the phone. Not every day, but let's say half of the days. When she does, she quickly replies with something. That is all I have going for me in my detective work. I do think when she does smile and reply, it would be to her admirer's text messages. What keeps hope in my bosom alive is, these messages are only intermittent. I tell myself that if she indeed is hooked to someone, texting would be incessant and she would steal looks at her phone even while she is working. I know I am engaging in fanciful thinking. But, my love for her is real. Well, that would make her only the 16th girl in my still fledgling life that I have felt a real love for.

The roads are super nice. I took five driving lessons. They are pretty expensive: $70 an hour. The instructor had a methodical way of teaching. Most of the time he kept urging me to slow down. I am driving around in a rented car on the weekends. There is traffic. I had thought the traffic problem would be non-existent in America. It turns out, that is not so. The main difference on the roads is, there is no two wheeler or pedestrian traffic. Incidentally, that reduces a lot of stress while driving. I find myself becoming a good driver. My colleagues caution me that the common mistake rookies make when they get a driving licence (by the way, it's called a driver's licence in this part of the world) is, they overspeed and end up getting tickets (the short hand for a fine by traffic cops). I don't imagine myself speeding over the prescribed limit, however. I am habitually cautious. I am planning to buy a car in a couple of months after I am paid in dollars for a few months. A used car is prohibitively expensive: a couple of months' salary should pay for it.

Before I arrived here, I had thought I would miss home terribly. That hasn't happened yet.

Maybe it's the newness of the place, maybe the comforts of it that have made me less nostalgic. Heck, let me be honest with you: I am not missing home at all. I had copied several hours of Hindi songs, lectures of great orators of India on CDs and had brought them with me in case I start weeping over India. I haven't had a chance to open those CDs yet. The days are not any more busy than they were in India. In fact, I have to spend less time on chores: I am hitting an Indian grocery store and stocking up on a lot of "ready-to-eat" curries. I cook rice by myself and a packet of an Indian side dish a day is serving me a royal meal each night. The novelties in life for a newcomer to America are endless. But, I will pause now from gushing over all of them in one go.

Please let me know how you are doing. How is College? Are the M.Sc. exams scheduled? Did you strike up a conversation with Karan? Do write to me everything that's happening in your life.

Love,
Akash

Chapter II. Tumult at Youth

Dear Akash,

I am at the crossroads of my life. I envy your freedom. Freedom from the shackles of parents. You are free to exercise your free will in the land of liberty. You can roam where you want, date who you want, eat what you want, and do what you want. My mother in particular is adamant that I get married soon. I want to complete my postgraduate degree, find a job, date a guy I like and then settle down. I just do not understand what is the hurry. Life as I understand it, doesn't end at 25. I will not suddenly become unmarriageable. The anguish I feel is maddening. I do not have mental space. And in the teeming city of Mumbai, I do not have physical space either. I do not mind sharing my flat with a thousand others. I do not want to share it with my parents, that's all. I wish I could join you in America. The other day I was to go to a birthday bash of a M.Sc. classmate. His name is Rohan. As these parties go, the party was to commence at 8 PM. Guess what? I wasn't allowed to go. While all my friends were enjoying the merry party, I was stuck at home. My mother is concerned about one thing and one thing only. That is, I shouldn't sleep with a guy. My question is, why not? All my girlfriends do. How am I so special that I shouldn't be allowed to do what a normal kid does? Anyway, I know I was ranting.

Thanks for the letter and the lovely description of what America is. It sure sounds like a dream land. I loved the bit about your dancing escapades. Feel free to ask the dazzling blonde dancing girl out! I will say, you still need to up your dating skills a bit. Here is my free advice: talk a little less about yourself, and be more curious about the woman. You will do fine. As to things concerning me, I did talk to Karan. He and I did have a couple of coffee dates. He is a nice chap. He is head over heels about me. I too initially thought he was cool. Of late, I am having second thoughts about him. I am mostly avoiding meeting him. He texts me incessantly. His sense of humor, literary flourish are a class apart. So I enjoy texting with him. I am loving keeping him at bay. The more I deny him, the more he feels motivated. Just when I think he has reached the pinnacles of his flirting prowess, he scales new heights. I only feel awe. So, I give him more room to grow. He has studied my routine minutely. Just last Monday, he made an

elaborate study schedule for my final exams
fitting in everything: the quirky TV shows I
watch, my coffee breaks. He had made a
crucial blunder though: he had slotted coffee
dates with him. I will use some of that time to
chat with him for his labors. But, coffee with
him? No, in his next life.

I told you that my mother wants to marry me
off as if I am a dead weight over her head that
she needs to shed. My folks arranged an
alliance date for me. I can't believe that people
can ever be that shoddy. The guy looks good
on paper. He is a business analyst at a
consulting firm in Mumbai. The crown jewel of
his life, which he made amply clear, was his
M.B.A. degree from a reputed college. He is
30. He has already bought a flat. He has an
older sister who is married. The four of them
came—the guy, his parents, and his sister. So
far, so good, isn't it? What's not to like about
the guy? Well, it turns out everything. I just do
not believe such retrograde people exist in
modern India and that too in modern Mumbai
still. He had worn a full length shirt, maybe
Peter England or something. It looked like the
whole lot of them had perfected the art of
barging in on unsuspecting girls' homes,
annoying the girls and wooing the parents

thoroughly. Ah, you should have seen that sheepish smile on the sister. God bless them. It was as though they were hunting for the prey like the legendary tiger in a cow's garb. If any girl falls for them, they will know how to butcher her. That was the impression I got anyway. They made all sweet talk. What enraged me the most was the inauthenticity of it all. The mother in a deadening sugary voice asks me how my studies are going. Mind you, I am meeting them for the first time in my life and ditto for them. How can you feign such closeness in the first meeting? It would be more appropriate to be a little somber and act normal. No girl wants to to be treated like she already is their daughter-in-law. I bet they won't treat me this nice if I fall for their trap. As you could expect, my folks fell for the theatrics. The father asks me, "Beta, can you cook?" What the heck. It panned out exactly how such classic visits go. Not a single variation. Everyone in their cohort has learned only perfectly how to read from the same script, act the same acts. Where is the innovation? Where is the individuality? If I was to pick one thing that put me off the most, I would certainly hand over the prize to that stupid cooking question. You know what I am going to say.

That the guy should actually marry his cook and call it a day.

It is not completely doom and gloom though. I too did go for Salsa classes. Before your imagination goes into an overdrive, let me state a simple fact for you: with my brother. He is fond of dancing too. As you know, he is two years older to me. We could have made a good couple if we were not born in the same mother's womb. Funny. It was fun. He is a solace to my otherwise troubled mind sometimes. He does not have a girlfriend. He is a perfect son for my parents. He toes their line, does their bidding. He is everything that they expect him to be. Unfortunately for them, they have begotten a thinking daughter. I don't know whose fault it is—theirs or mine. Sometimes he tries to keep peace between them and me. I am just glad there is somebody who stands by me—my brother. The plan thus far is, I am married off first and then they will look for a suitable bride for him. It boggles my mind to no end, why everyone is so bent on having perfect lives. Perfection is overrated, if you ask me. I am finding it curative to express to you what I am feeling. It is cathartic.

I have taken up serious biking. It's wonderful. Long distance biking is helping me keep myself fit. What's more, when I am riding outside the hustle and bustle of the city, and going through the verdant countryside, I feel liberated. Most of the time, my mind is empty, which is fantastic. I have heard (but do not want to experiment), when you are in a deep meditation, you feel a sense of emptiness. Through my biking, I achieve the same. When the mind is not empty, I feel only happy thoughts. I feel I am unshackled and free. You can give it a shot too, even if you are not anguished. I have joined an online bikers' group on Facebook. It is there that people organize these expeditions mostly composed of strangers. Only a subset of people that have signed up for any ride, show up while others don't. It's better to ride in a group than alone. It's safer. Since I don't know anybody there that closely, I keep to myself. It's working out perfectly for me. On a recent Sunday we rode all the way down to Pune and back. Since it was just past the Monsoon season, the beauty of the stretch between Mumbai and Pune was breathtaking. Living in the city, you don't realize how the landscape changes for the better just a few kilometres from here. I loved every second of it. We left at 5.30 AM and returned at around 9 PM. It was a long ride. When I came back home, I was dead. I just ate and hit the sack and didn't wake up until 10 AM the next morning. The ride itself was great. Until the last stretch when we were entering Mumbai, I didn't feel tired. I didn't know I could ride such long distances. Evidently, I could and did.

My friends' plights are not far better. Every girl I know has one or the other irritant to face, major or minor. Trupti who was my best friend in school, who you used to fancy when she used to visit my home often, is in the middle of a messy divorce. She got married (or was married off) at a young age. She and her husband had a baby son too. That baby is two years old now. Their marriage hit a rough patch. She is currently living with her parents. She wants some monetary settlement from her husband. Her husband I feel is OK. His parents are veritable Satans. They are moneyed people. They have hired a criminal lawyer (who I have heard is more like a goonda) and are harassing Trupti and her folks. Then, there is Preksha. She is insufferable. She doesn't know what she wants in life. She calls me up once in a while and when she calls you, you can bet, she has called only to cry. Her problems appear flimsy to me—both her parents are medical doctors.

She says they want her to enroll in Medicine even after she has done her B.Sc. I tell her, well tell them that you don't want to. She says, she can't and that she fears them and that if she speaks her mind to them, all hell will break loose. I have never met her parents. I don't know if her parents are that scary or it is only in her mind. I will be remiss if I don't tell you about the queen of drama queens: Reshma. She keeps contradicting herself in the same sentence. She is with a guy. That guy is good—I have seen him, have talked to him. She has imaginary complaints about him—he takes his orders from his mama, his mama is a monster and he is too tall. I think she needs to be given a prize for coming up with the most creative gripes. They were to get hitched. Now, she is coming up with these kinds of grievances. I told her, "Break up with him. You guys aren't married yet". To which she says, that's not possible. Why? Because she has told her parents about him and that her mother has spoken to his mother once over the phone. I am lost for words for such unreasonable behavior. God bless her and that guy. For good measure, I would say, his mama too if my friend takes a leap of faith to make her her mother-in-law.

The finances of my household are a bit out of order right now. Papa was doing quite well in the garment industry. He had bought a cotton mill and had an associated tailoring house too. He was selling men's and women's wear both in India and abroad. Papa being papa thought he could do better. He sold the garment business and ventured into pharmaceuticals. He thought he could make more money. I can never understand him. If things are going well, it starts bothering him. Inevitably, pharma being new to him, he is struggling. He also says he underestimated the cutthroat competition in the pharma business. Because India is a pharma powerhouse and the revenues are big, there genuinely is a tough competition. There are entrenched players and those who have figured out how to make a complex enterprise come together. I think for papa, pharma having inherently having more moving parts than garments, it has thus far been a tough nut to crack. It saddens me to see him struggling thus. I hardly see him during the week. On Sundays, he makes it a point to stay home. The rest of the days, I don't even know when he returns home. His face is sagged and the worry is writ large on his face. But, I do give him credit for never shying away from challenges. I sincerely hope he gets his mooring right soon. We are pulling along with good savings that papa had made from the past several years. If he starts sinking much money in the new venture, then before long the going might indeed get tough for day-to-day expenses too. Mom is shouldering the whole burden of running the show at home and keeping papa's spirits up. Her forbearance is God-level. I don't know if I would have been able to take what I would consider unnecessary worry for my husband if I had a husband like papa. I know under the surface she is dispirited too, but outwardly she is not betraying even an iota of her inner turmoil. She is shielding papa 100% from domestic strife. I think secretly she too had been saving money. I guess knowing papa as she did, she must have reckoned such a day would indeed come to pass. She is dipping into such slush funds and running the household freeing papa mostly from having to contribute to daily expenses as well. I don't know for sure.

Karan is keeping me good company. I share with him everything. If you were here, maybe I could have leaned on your shoulder for a good cry. Alright, he is a bit more intelligent than you, truth be told. He acts serious when I am relaying serious stories. Then he is back to square one—offering to take me out for dinner, cinema and what have you. I think he lives in his own fantasy world where I am his girlfriend and he is a multi-millionaire. His hopes towards me never dim even after I tell him that I have zero interest in having him as my boyfriend. He thinks it's only a matter of time before I relent. No, seriously not. I wish I could let him see that what I harbor for him doesn't remotely touch the ring of romance. It truly does not. The good part of it is, he is sensible. When I am not in a mood to respond, he does not pester and does not stalk (physically at least, which is super important). I guess I am missing having a boyfriend, somebody who I could rely on completely for everything. Someone who would be my partner to share the grief and joys of day-to-day life. A guy who I have feelings for. You know what I am talking about. Yeah, I can never seem to get him out of my mind. It has been quite a while—a few months at least since I last saw him. I do not know how one can flip flop on these matters. After I confessed my love for him (which has been there for eternity), he was overjoyed. He said he loved me too. Then suddenly, he comes around and says, he is sure things won't work out. Why? I have harassed you on these details umpteen number of times. He said, he and his people are poorer than me and my people. I wish he knew how we are struggling financially at this very moment. Somehow even if I tell him that, I know what he will say: unbridgeable gaps in our status levels remain. I have no clue what he is talking about. What good has come out of his watching as many Bollywood movies as he has watched if he thinks love cannot surpass such temporary, artificial barriers? In fact, they don't exist in our case. And, that brings me to inform you that I have hatched a plan for the express purpose of winning the love of my life. I am going to give it a last push and see what happens. I hope it succeeds with every ounce of living force within me. I cannot think of the alternative. It's too unthinkable, so I am not going to dwell on it. Here is the plan: his mother is known to me. I am pretty certain she is well disposed towards me. I will take her into confidence. If she gives her blessing, Amol will come around. Once he is on board, I will broach the subject with my folks. Papa especially I think will be quite opposed to what I will have to say. He is too focused on class, wealth, and status. Ah, Amol was not really off the mark. But, I will not sacrifice my life at the altar of some imaginary honor of my father! At any rate, I haven't come to that bridge yet to cross. For all you know, papa might just say OK. Who knows? To mix things up a bit, it could be my mother who might come up with some ruse to not make it happen. Because of this planning that has been going on in my head, I have been feeling quite hopeful lately. To tell you the truth, I am darn excited about just netting that guy than actually living with him. When you are denied something, it raises your desire to obtain it more. Our minds are strange in that way.

That is what is up with me. I am feeling so good right now. It's as though you are still here. We are distant now and God knows for how long we will be. It helps to know that you are still there. You have been someone who has been more than a friend. I haven't had a chance to express to you what you have meant for me. I wanted to say, you are like a brother. That is not exactly true. You are a friend. Probably, English lexicon doesn't have a correct phrase for what we share. Maybe, "alter ego" fits the bill? I will let you think about it. Now that you are in America, I will let you be the English judge. I keep tripping over myself —you are an American judge! Do write to me soon.

Love,
Saroja

Chapter III. American Dream

Dear Saroja,

I was heavenly pleased to read your letter. I think when you are happy, everything that happens to you looks and feels like a godsend. That is to say, I am happy. For the record, receiving your letter always adds to joy, whether I am happy or not. First of all, I would like to reciprocate your sentiment on our friendship. You are the only one that I express myself to, as freely as I do. So, much thanks for that.

Coming to America and seeing how everything runs here, I daresay, has changed my perspective. I think, the adage that "Life is short. Don't waste it on remorse." is not an empty sentiment. I see less sentimentality in American life and I am wholeheartedly embracing it myself. In America, a girl can dump a guy one day, find a new one to move on with the next day and to move in with the day after. I guess Americans do cry, they too feel the weight of love and break-ups, but they don't dwell on it. I think that is the crucial difference between how you and I have been habitually conditioned from childhood and how Americans grow up imbibing the values from what they witness around them. That sets the stage for what I wanted to do as soon as I folded your letter: admonish you. Amol. How long have you not been attempting to make him realize that you both will live happily ever after if only he deigns to come down and meet you not halfway but at his own doorsteps? It has been what, five years now? Why don't you just move on? You know you can get another guy who is better in every respect. Why waste your energy and emotions on someone who doesn't realize who is coming knocking on his door? I have little patience for your mawkish stories now than ever before. Please, please, for God's sake, don't cry over him. That is not worth a single tear of yours. I know the disclaimer I am going to write is really unnecessary. But, don't let the distance (the physical distance anyway) make you not see that I have the noblest of intentions for you. Further, I want to make it amply clear: I did not mean that you should not write to me about Amol. You are more than welcome to write your heart out. In fact, that is what I will most ardently be looking forward to. I only wanted to let you know how I feel about the entire story. It's up to you, of course.

Let's see if my cheery stories of America do anything to cheer you up. Ever since I have set foot on the American soil, it has been a dream run for me. Do you remember the cartoons you and I used to watch as children? Beautiful gardens, well laid out houses, snow-capped mountains as though a great artist had just painted them on TV. That is America for you. Wherever I see, it exudes beauty. I feel hesitant to step onto the road, step into a house lest I disturb the perfect neatness of their states. I continually marvel how they could keep it so well groomed. It's not as though it's cleaned up, immaculately arranged for a special occasion. It's an everyday affair. I can't stop loving it. I recently bought a car. A Mercedes-Benz. I was always into cars. Driving in my Merc feels divine. Zooming past 100 miles an hour on broad, smooth roads ought to give one a feel of being transported to a magical world. Material prosperity oozes from every corner of this vast country. Overstuffed supermarkets, mansion-like suburban houses, garden-like lawns in front of each house, steady sunshine, clean cars, silent environs, terrific beauty of nature. You have got to wonder if this isn't a paradise. I should add that beautiful girls that look like angels abound too. I had dreamed of landing in America some day, but I couldn't have imagined if my dream place would induce such dreaminess in me. I have signed onto a dating App and keep sending likes to every woman. I am happy to report I have had some matches too. On a couple of occasions I went to sip coffee too with charming belles. I did OK I think although I don't think we clicked. In case you are wondering, it's not as though you go on a date and you get laid the same night. It takes time here too. Women everywhere are a bit of tough nuts to crack. I am certain I will succeed in my objects one of these days.

As good as things are, I am feeling too lonely. After office hours and on weekends, I have the time in my hands which I do not have anyone to spend with. I miss the office banter I used to have with my co-workers in India. The work culture here is more professional. All everyone talks about in the office is work. Occasionally, they share small stories about where they went, what they did on the weekends, but that's mostly during lunch breaks or near the coffee machine. Everyone comes in just after 8 in the morning and heads home by 4. They have less time to dilly dally. I had a couple of close buddies at work in Mumbai—Ajit and Sukrut. We used to play pool together, talk about girls, review movies and more. All three of us being gf-less, and wife-less, we used to hang out in the office cafeteria till 8 in the evening. I lack that camaraderie. In the fiercely individualistic culture of the West, I, who is accustomed to chit-chatting with those around me, am having a tough time to reconfigure my being. I grew so desperate for company last Sunday that I walked to the office hoping somebody must have shown up. It was as deserted as a town after a nuclear holocaust. One lady showed up with her dog. I think she just wanted to walk her dog. I said "hi" to her hoping to start a conversation. She nervously smiled and went about her business. I felt like a fool. I think that it's not just me who feels lonely around here. While I was walking back from the Indian grocery store closest to my place the other day, I saw a man, not probably older than me, in fact slightly younger, just sitting at the bus stop. I didn't know what to make of him. I felt he was a bit shady. It was nearing 9 PM. I wondered why he was still sitting there. Wouldn't his mother and father be waiting for him at home? If I were in Mumbai, I couldn't loiter around and certainly not sit around in a bus stop late at night without triggering a panic back at my home. I don't know. Maybe, he lives alone. Maybe, he is homeless! Yes, people are homeless here too. Their plight is actually worse than those of homeless people in India. I would say not least because of the loneliness that they face. In India, homeless people too have families. For better or worse, they are in it together. Here, homeless people are singletons. I wonder if homeless people could just band together and create supporting structures for themselves. No. I have witnessed them fighting with each other. It's scary. If there is an underbelly to an otherwise paradise-like America, it is this. I am new to America. I do not feel displaced, not as yet anyway. That is one thing I worry—if I belong here. The other day I saw a group of what appeared to be high school pals hanging out. Two boys, two girls. I couldn't clearly make out what they were talking so excitedly about. Maybe movies, maybe teachers, or maybe philosophy. I couldn't help but think, how far away from home I have come. It reminded me of myself with you and our clique in our own heydays. It's their land, it's their place. I, who is surely not shunned, but still feel like an alien. In fact, that's the formal designation the U.S. government bestows on me: a foreign alien.

I am not writing this letter to you in one sitting.
I come back to write to you when I miss you
the most, when I want to tell you what's going
on as though you are here, or I am still there.
You are my conduit to the outside world. In
these pages, I pen my deepest thoughts. You
are non-judgmental. You are my safe place.
After I told you about the scourge of loneliness
I was facing, I had not been home for several
days. I returned just today. I went to Vegas,
Las Vegas. I came across a bunch of like
minded people—3 guys, 2 girls who are my
age and who asked me if I wanted to join them
on a Vegas trip. Thus it happened. It's the sin
city of the world. Strippers, gorgeous strippers
at that flock to Vegas to make a quick buck. It
was funny. I didn't indulge in any serious sin. A
part of the reason was the company I had
been with. They were good boys. I wish they
had made a better company. Anyway, I didn't
gamble, didn't get laid, but still had a lot of fun.
The tourist guides only half jokingly say, it's
the only city in the world that's visible from
outer space. That's how bright it is at night!
When we were landing down at the Vegas
airport late in the evening, I could for miles and
miles see only neon lights. You got to wonder,
how they placed a city that bright and big in
the middle of a desert. The company of the

friends I had been with was good, notwithstanding their aversion to sin. I liked a girl. She is Indian. Her name is Kanika. She lives in San Francisco. She was one of the members of our crew. I was chit chatting with a guy. I was animatedly shooting down his points of view, for fun. I didn't believe an iota of what I was saying. She clearly was eavesdropping. In the middle of our conversation, she joined in and had a rejoinder to what I had said. I just gave her a curious look and didn't reply. I was hesitant to start talking to her lest she think I am a creep. She is stunningly beautiful. Her eyes with mascara on are bewitching. Whenever I thought she was not looking in my direction, my eyes invariably darted towards her. I just couldn't take my eyes off her for all the four days that I had the time to spend with her. Slowly, we started talking. I kept close to her. She didn't seem to mind. She didn't dismiss me as too eager a guy to keep distance from. Once I realized that she was comfortable with me being around, I felt no need to hide my admiration for her. I was like her Personal Assistant. When she said, she is thirsty, I would go on a trot and fetch water for her. One night, she said, she wanted to go see the Strip again—the thoroughfare that has the largest casinos in Vegas. She had addressed her wish generally to everyone. I, who was ever eager to please her, said, I would go. It so happened that no one else was interested. It was only she and me who went out at 11 PM. It felt like I was living out a most beautiful romantic story. There was a bit of a crowd at some point along the stretch. Instinctively I held her hand. We walked like a couple that whole night. That's what I most remember about this trip: Kanika. I thought it was a charming trip. She lives some hundreds of miles away from where I live. I have got her phone number. I am not sure if I should call. I want her memory to be etched in my mind the way I am feeling about her right now—in the most affectionate terms. I don't know if long distance romance would be satisfying or will even work out. But, I have a deeper fear: what if I have read too much into her attitude towards me. What if she has not looked at me as nothing more than a passing friend? As kind and tender she was towards me, what if it is her natural demeanor? I do not know if calling her up is a good idea. I think I will not.

The routine has set in. The more I look around, the more I see things as unremarkable. Curiously, I am missing Mumbai crowds. How can one suddenly forget 25 years of one's life? I cannot. How can I reconcile myself to live in a heap of luxury when my people are not here to partake in it? Tears are rolling down my cheeks as I am writing this. I miss you. I miss everything. I just want to be home. The roads are big, but vehicles are sparse. The houses are grand, but people are few. Life is smooth, but the mind is in a tumult. And, the root cause is, there is not a soul around whom I can call my own. That is my state. I had dreamed of coming to America ever since I can remember. When I got a chance to land here through a work assignment, I was overjoyed. The initial days were a haze of ecstasy and mirth. The excitement is wearing off. I am beginning to see that life here has its own set of shortcomings too. Apart from being scores of thousands of miles away from my near and dear ones, life in America entails a lot of hard work, especially at home. The domestic help is non-existent. I have to cook my own food, do my dishes myself, launder my clothes myself, and clean my house with my own hands. The immaculate looking houses, the gleaming roads are no accident. The dust here is no less virulent. It dirties the surfaces just the same as it does in Mumbai. It's through sheer hard work that it is wiped clean, and scrubbed to perfection. That's my epiphany after spending a few months in the promised land. In a way, it's good too: I am becoming self reliant. In Mumbai, I didn't know how to make my own coffee. I am rivalling a chef now. I can cook pretty much everything: rice, daal, sabji are mundane. I can make gulab jamuns, pasta, and put together a yummy Mexican burrito too. I never realized the value of maids and cooks in India. I thought what they did were menial jobs. I see they are anything but menial. There is a certain beauty in seeing the dosas come out crispy while its fragrance is wafting through the air. There is a particular sense of accomplishment in seeing your apartment shining clean again after an hour's back breaking work. I jokingly think to myself that whoever marries me would be so lucky for she would have got a perfect chef, a cleaner, and not to mention a hunk all in one.

I have taken up Tennis. There is a sports Club near where I live. I took some five lessons and now I can hold the racket steady and return a few of the shots that land in my court. I am liking it. There is a forum to find willing hitting partners. I was paired with one Allie. She is probably two years younger to me. She is finishing up her college. She is phenomenal. I often think if she signs up to play in the professional women's Tennis circuit, she can be a champion already. I don't know why she doesn't consider that. I have to ask her. She is a little shorter than me. She is a white Caucasian girl. She is stunningly good looking. I admire her immensely. But, as far my interactions with her go, I don't engage in anything other than Tennis with her. We hardly talk. We show up on the court at a pre-agreed time and just start hitting. The girls in America are brought up slightly differently I would think: they beat the heck out of you. They are not told, "if you are a girl, you can't do this or that". They can do everything. She is too good. Her forehands are ferocious, and the backhands untouchable. I am really lousy as a Tennis partner for her. Still, when I call her up to ask if she would like to play, she doesn't baulk. She shows up to the Club all the same. Solely to give her a good time, I am working on my Tennis skills with double the effort. I am improving. On our fifth meeting, she couldn't contain her glee. She came to the net and yelled, "You are getting a lot better", with a beautiful grin on her face. My heart swelled with joy and pride. Ah, what wouldn't I do to see that mischievous smile on her face again? Once instead of calling her up on her phone, I emailed her asking if she is up for a Tennis date that evening. She replied "OK". I was much baffled to see the name that popped up when her email hit my inbox: "Alexandra Blackburn". I had all along thought that her name was just "Allie". Then, I realized Alexandra is abbreviated as Allie. Then when we met, I asked her "Alexandra is your name then?" with a knowing smile on my face. It was like she was holding onto a secret all that while. That's how I felt anyway. In India, sometimes you have a very long name that you don't feel particularly proud of, and hence, you go by a fancier shorter version of it before your friends. One fine day however, you are outed. That's how I felt about the emergence of Alexandra from Allie. That was the smile I was wearing when I asked her that question. She also reciprocated. She also had that smile that showed me that she wasn't particularly fond of her given name either. That was the ice-breaker. Interestingly, that eased my demeanor around her. I felt freer. The culture barrier that existed between her and me broke down. I came to know I can tease her and elicit a girly response. She knew I had her number too. Strangely, we felt connected over her name! A name that is as unremarkable to her as anything that she grew up with and a name that was as mysterious to me as America was. Her familiarity and my foreignness to a name ushered in a gust of warmth between us, who otherwise were separated by a gulf of differences. I think I flirted with her a little after the game. She was only giggling throughout. I even asked if she was interested in watching a Bollywood movie with me. She said, hold your breath, "yes".

Love,
Akash

Chapter IV. Initial Adjustment

Dear Akash,

I am getting married. Yes! And, getting married to Amol. It was a miracle that it came together. When I was feeling hopeless and had thought I would never be able to consummate the love of my life, it just happened. The stars have to align for everything. I would be a fool to say, it was my doing. It was not. I am also perplexed how everything fell in place in the end. Alright, that's just too many words expressing my awe without explaining anything. Here we go.

In my last letter I told you that Amol was flip-flopping and his mother had a gracious attitude towards me. I was thinking of bringing her onboard in our marriage saga and I was hoping that that would set a chain of events that would lead to my marriage with Amol. Things turned out slightly differently. It was a holiday and papa and I were driving. It was a casual drive. He likes to take drives. This time he asked me if I would like to join him. Mother was busy with something. Brother was not at home. So, only he and I went. We drove some 120 km north of Mumbai. While returning, he asked me if I like someone. It was a question out of the blue. Nothing had happened recently that would have aroused his curiosity either (because I was not seeing anyone as you know). To that sudden question, I merely blurted out "Yes". The next question naturally from him was, "Who?" I told him it was Amol. He seemed to recall him. He said, "Oh the boy from your school?" I was amazed that he remembered. I said, "Yeah". At this point, I thought it was getting serious and awkward. He pressed on: "Weren't you guys in the same play once? You were Radha and he was Krishna". I said that was true too. I haven't confessed this to you also: that it was when I first started having feelings towards him. Call it a divine plan, if you will. He took it most casually. He said that was good and asked me how it was progressing. By this time, I had felt there was no resistance from Papa and in fact, I thought he was on my side. I felt like sharing with him my sob story. He appeared touched by it. He asked me if it would help if he talked to his folks. I said, "Really? That would be wonderful". The next day, he called up (from his office) his mother. He talked to her and Amol's father. It seemed that they were only overjoyed to hear from him. They had believed that he would be a roadblock to Amol's marriage with me if it ever got to that stage. His mother had always liked me. His father was also privy to the goings-on, it emerged. Now, the only person left to be talked to and be convinced was the poor prince-charming himself. He is close to his mother. They are like friends. I sometimes feel jealous of his mother because he talks to her so much and confides in her everything. In this instance though that proved to be a blessing. Being intimate, her words mollified him and the fear stricken Amol was unshackled from the imaginary handcuffs he had worn himself. When he called me four days after my talk to my father, he was most happy and most pleasing. It's like we had never stopped talking. It felt so natural. I know this is so devoid of drama, the drama that one would have expected in such situations. As I said, even I can't believe it. How could it have been so easy? Think of the odds of it happening: my dad would want to go on a drive, only me joining him, him asking me that question about liking someone, I in a moment of unguarded honesty answering him truthfully, him without a second thought seeming to take pity on me. Not only that, him then phoning his parents up. I hope I didn't jinx it by saying what I said. I hope before long he and I would get to live as husband and wife. Bless me, Akash. Bless us!

The recent days have been crazily busy. I am working hard preparing for my M.Sc. exams. I don't want to flunk a subject or two just before my wedding you see. No, seriously I am putting in quite a lot of work. The initial excitement of getting to live with the love of my life is giving way to the anxiety about the future. I think I am already thinking like a wife. Amol is not particularly rich. He is a Sales associate for a government insurance company. Although I believe he would ever lose his job, his income would never be huge either. So, it has become all the more important that I find a job and find it soon. Hence, the hard work for the upcoming exams. If I do well, then I will hopefully be able to find a good paying job and we can live a decent life. My best friend—Archana let it slip that I could have found a rich husband with my looks and all. That made me turn and toss in my bed for two days in a row. On the third day, it just occurred to me that I wouldn't have wanted it any other way. I want to live with him. I want to grow with him. I want to die with him. Really, the material wealth had never interested me greatly. Who can refuse a good dollop of money if it comes your way? I can't either. But, I won't deliberately go looking for it. I like Amol for his magnificent mind. He is not the most brilliant of minds I have known. In fact, in that respect Karan is superior. Karan, who was bugging me with his lyrical serenades is many times more intelligent than Amol. Probably, Karan will grow leaps and bounds in his career too. Never once did that tempt me away from Amol. What I like most about Amol is his level headedness and kindness. I have seen it umpteen number of times in him. His natural instincts inclined towards the noble traits make him act in an admirable manner even when no one is looking. He doesn't care if anybody is looking or not. He doesn't act to gain anybody's attention or to earn accolades. In school, once there was a girl who was bullied and shunned by other kids. The reason? She had bunny teeth. Amol went out of his way and befriended her. This was much before I had started loving him. At that stage, my only feeling towards him was that of respect. He would have lunch with her. The cool friends of Amol wanted nothing to do with the girl. They sat as far away from them as possible. But, that didn't faze him. This went on for three years. When we reached grade eight, that girl went somewhere else. Only then did Amol feel free to resume the company of his cool friends once more. His friends were most welcoming of him again. He carried that majesty with him.

Nobody dared to make fun of him. There was conviction in his heart. Everybody feared that. That is the aura that I eventually fell in love with. If there is a flaw in him, I would think it's complacency. As you very well know, I was the queen bee of my class. There was no dearth of guys circling around me. But, it is me who desired him. He later confessed that he had his eyes on me too. He didn't really fall over himself to woo me. It came together quite naturally. Even recently, he didn't want to marry me or more correctly, he didn't want me to marry him because he didn't want me to suffer a loss of comforts in life. That is what he told me. He said, he never doubted his worth, but that he may not be able to afford me the life I have lived in my father's home. He didn't exactly say that in those words. However, that is what I have gathered after probing him, putting two and two together ever since we have been hanging out again. It's pure bliss to be with him. I love him with all my heart. No, I wouldn't have been happier if I had married a tycoon.

I am slowly coming to realize that there are many expectations of me. Amol is the oldest of the kids. He has a younger brother and a much younger sister. I am expected to be the big sister to both of them. It's not only him that I will marry. I will marry his entire family. It's daunting. Having a good life with him is a breeze. Having a harmonious life with all his family is the challenge before me. In my home, I was the youngest and I was brought up like a small kid the whole time. Now, all of a sudden I will be the oldest and believed to be the wisest of the children in my new home. I am feeling totally inadequate. Amol is not helping. He only says, I will do fine. Easy for him to say that. His nonchalance is getting on my nerves. Nobody seems to think that my fears are worth a serious consideration. My mother patiently listens and launches into how she managed when she came to papa's house. As interesting as that story might be, that is not helping me one bit. My father is a bit more understanding but has no practical advice to offer. So, it's left to me to find a solution to my problem. That anxiety has been keeping me up at night. I do not know why others are unable to grasp what I am anxious of. Maybe, after a few months in his home I will find my footing again and all that I am feeling now may look silly even to me then. Or maybe not. I guess, I have to just bite the bullet and see what happens. The die has been cast. Now, there is no turning back. That is how my days have been—worrying half the time, talking to him a quarter of the time, studying the rest of the time. The wedding preparations have to pick up steam. It's four months away. See if you can make it to our wedding. If you cannot, I will completely understand.

I am back to writing to you again. The countdown to the wedding has begun. Each passing day feels like the countdown to a mega blast. I am using the word -- blast in both of its senses—it will be fun and like a bomb blast, bruising. I went out shopping with Amol's younger sister. She had just written her tenth board exams. She is a chatterbox. I love her. The whole time, she was telling me the stories of her life. "Didi, didi" never stopped coming out of her mouth. She really looks up to me. When I came back home, I closed the door to my room and cried. I don't know if I can do justice to my role of being a big sister to her. She is so innocent and full of dreams. After interacting with her, I realized our sense of age is totally distorted. We think, or at least I thought, that people who are older to you know better. Increasingly, that is appearing to be a fallacy. They know no better. Or, more specifically I know no better than his sister does. She was asking me if she should choose

Science stream or Commerce stream after tenth standard. She was marveling how I can read up books as thick as I have for my M.Sc program. She was saying I must be a genius. I tried to explain to her, I am nothing of the sort, I am only an ordinary person. To which she would say, I am humble too. It was not irritating at all because her feelings and awe were genuine. Then, she went on to describe how Amol acts differently when I am around. That revelation was new to me and it warmed my heart. Apparently, when I am visiting their house, he is his best self. He has a tendency to burp after a meal it seems but when I am around he suppresses it. I didn't know that. So, after I leave, all his family pokes fun at his altered manners when his heartthrob comes over. This little girl went on to say, she had always dreamt of having a big sister and my marrying Amol is making that dream come true. I was touched by that. Strangely I realized when I talk to Amol that I am not talking to him alone but indirectly to a whole set of people—his family. Often he relays good things I say about his folks to them. I had told Amol that I liked his mama's sari. I had especially liked the maroon red color of it and the designs on it. He faithfully debriefed his mother about it. And, his mother suggested that they will buy a similar sari for me for the wedding. All of it was to be a surprise save the little girl's candid admission. I must say, I am relaxing a bit. His family are just normal people too. They are not some devils that will pounce on me the moment I enter their house. They are a normal, and sometimes a squabbling family like mine after all. They have similar dreams and anxieties as everyone else I guess. What's more, they are looking forward to welcoming me. I don't know if they have thought if I will bring a sea change in their lives. I am excited too. Their family will gain a new member and I, a whole new family.

As excited as Amol's folks are for my arrival, my folks are equally morose. The reality is sinking for my mother and father, I think that I am leaving them before long. My papa is more affected. Every day when he comes back home from work, he makes it a point to chat with me for a half hour. On and off we used to chat before too, but now he consciously seeks me out and finds topics to talk to me about. If he can't think of anything else, he has figured the safest way to open a conversation is to throw the question "What's the latest with Amol?" Sometimes, I cannot help but sense the shaking tenor in his voice. He quickly recovers and pretends everything is fine. I am not exactly ecstatic too for leaving them behind. But, I guess, for me it's a double edged sword—I am losing something and gaining something else. For them, it's only losing. In that sense, they are more affected by it. The good part is, I won't be far away. So, I can visit them as often as I want and as often as they want. It's not as though I am flying away to a different part of the world (like you). I will be right here, in the next neighborhood. While I am thinking about it, I cannot ever imagine living in a place halfway across the world. I admire your courage. Now, I am beginning to appreciate what you had to give up to pursue your dreams. I don't know if you feel about it exactly the same way as I do (maybe not), but still from my perspective, your courage stands tall. I cannot brook not being around my family for any extended period of time, while you I presume will go on not seeing your parents for years on end. Regardless of everything else, that elicits in me a newfound admiration for you. You have broken away from the bonds that bind us from birth and are after something greater in life. Even though I cannot ever emulate you, know that I will always view your pursuit of grander goals in life with awe.

The wedding date is woefully close. In a week's time by next week this time, God willing, I will be married to Amol. A new chapter of my life will open. Everything is a haze right now. The dread of it has absolutely terrified me. I am like a zombie. I am just shambling around not knowing exactly what I am doing. But, it's great. The D-Day had to arrive at some point. I am glad it's happening on my own terms. I count myself lucky. Probably you can sense that I am in a panic, mumbling incoherent thoughts. Everything is set. The wedding hall was booked long ago. I chose the floral decorations for the marriage hall. I chose a combination of chrysanthemum and rose petals for the background decorations—right behind where Amol and I will be sitting beaming (or crying) at the crowd. Papa, mama are in the same state as I am, probably worse. At best, my role is to only do what I am told. It's on them to arrange everything. I haven't been able to talk to Amol much in the last 3–4 weeks well. I am saving our conversations for later. After all, we will have a whole lifetime to sort out our thoughts together, will we not? My best friend—Archana is camping with me in my home most days. She has absolutely been a delight. If it were not for her, I would have lost my mind by now.

When somebody asks me a question, I have to first run it by her to translate the question for me. Each word I hear sounds garbled. She patiently explains what is expected of me. I just do it. By the way, we are off to Mauritius two days after the wedding. I was telling Amol the other day how you are enjoying the time of your life in Seattle. He knew you, but not very well. He wants to meet you when you come down here next. I want to too. Take care. See if you can convince Allie to marry you. Your American Dream will be complete. Bye.

Love,
Saroja

Chapter V. Better to Best

Dear Saroja,

Heartiest congratulations to you and Amol. I do not know Amol well enough to compliment you as I am going to compliment him: without a shadow of a doubt, he is the luckiest man in the world. When I read your beautiful letter and learned of the impending wedding, my heart swelled with happiness and I have to admit, my eyes became moist. A wedding is the most solemn occasion in anyone's life. I am glad and I am overwhelmed with a gush of goodwill towards you and Amol. Even though I wouldn't be able to be there to bless you both in person, know that my best wishes travel the seven oceans to reach you to greet you on the big day and for a lifetime to come.

I am at the crossroads of life myself too. I am doing very well professionally. Less than a year into the job, I got promoted and now I am the Vice President of Data Analytics in my company. I go before the C.E.O on a regular basis and brief him on our data strategy. A lot of the knowledge base I had built up over the years is coming handy now. In fact, I couldn't have become the V.P. if it were not for the midnight oil I burned learning exotic concepts out of curiosity earlier. In some sense, I feel vindicated. My passion was directed well after all. Money is a second thought now. Truth be told, with the new position that I have ascended, in a year's time I will have amassed enough wealth to settle for a retired life in India. No kidding. Yet, my ambition is burning brighter than ever. On the personal front, I am dating Allie now. I might soon pop the question to her: "Will you marry me?".

Yet, something is missing. Outwardly, I am everything that a decent guy anywhere in the world would aspire to be. To be clear, I am not going through a spiritual crisis. I have Allie by my side. My parents are doing OK in the remote lands of India. But, I have this ineffable pain somewhere in the corner of my soul. I can't put a finger on it. I have a feeling it has to do with displacement. As much as America holds the allure for me, I miss India. Although I know it is filthy, crowded, and filled with mean spirited people, I long for it. On some nights without warning I start hallucinating. The dreams turn into nightmares. On one such night, I woke up to remember what had caused the sweat in the middle of the night: I was sitting in a mansion all alone and there was no one around me. It clearly looked like I was an old man then. Probably, that is what is bothering me I think: that I will die alone. Yeah, I know: this is no age to die, no age to think of death either. Maybe, that's the real hidden terror that's playing tricks on my mind. I do not know how to overcome it. That imagined horrific end hasn't burst out of the blue after all. There is a good chance that that will be my fate in this foreign land which I have made my own. The solution: a marriage and bountiful children to not make that come true. When I write to you, things in fact become clearer for me too.

Allie proposed that we go visit her family. I felt jubilant. She hails from Michigan. Her parents are farmers. She is one of seven children to them. Yeah, they are a big family. I readily agreed to travel down to Michigan. We have to travel East and a bit South to reach there from Seattle. We took a few days off work (she has finished College and is a working woman now) and decided to drive instead of flying. It was great fun driving through the beautiful and vast countryside. I loved the remote village her folks inhabit in. The houses there are quite far apart. Their nearest neighbor is some three miles away. When I entered their big farm house, it felt like I was stepping into eighteenth century England. My understanding of England comes from English authors of course—Charles Dickens, and Jane Austen mainly. I was just awed and mesmerized by the whole surroundings. They had a ringing wind chime outside the main door that would chime at all hours of the day and the soothing sounds emanating from it at night especially were enchanting. There was a piano that girls of the family would start playing in the evenings impromptu. Allie is also a good piano player. She claims her younger sister plays it the best. I am not endowed with a gifted ear to ascertain, but I hear maestro's music all around be it from Allie or her sister. Her father and mother were kind to me and treated me well. As much as they attempted to conceal it, I couldn't help but sense their anxiety for their daughter with regards to her future with me. On many occasions, they were toning down their English to make sure I was able to understand it. I so much wanted to tell them to not worry—even though I might still speak in an accent slightly different from the American twang, I am second to none when it comes to the prowess over that ancient language. Allie of course knows it. What I found quite surprising was, a seemingly formal relationship Allie shares with her parents. It's a lot superficial. Unlike your and my interactions with our parents, she is more reserved with her folks. Her conversations with her parents are more like our talks with our aunts and uncles. Hence, she couldn't forcefully press my case with them. She couldn't admonish them for thinking that I am second to her in many ways. Their notion of India is also, I have to regretfully admit, is quite antiquated. Their understanding of India comes from their local pastor, who I also had the misfortune of meeting. Her family are regular Church goers. Allie and I accompanied them to the Sunday mass. Curiously, I was the only foreigner in their midst. Many of the "villagers" or officially considered townspeople would come up to me and say a few kind words as though I might at that very moment be starving and suffering from third-world famines and diseases. That was bothersome. When they learned that I had come there as Allie's boyfriend, their faces would sag and they would cast pitiful looks in the direction of Allie as if some demon had addled her mind. I couldn't wait for our three days of planned visit to end. Speaking of the pastor, he told me he spent four years in India when he was barely a teenager. Why? He said, his father was a missionary in Assam at the time. He apparently had picked up quite a bit of Assamese too. His impression of India was sadly not much brighter than those of his parishioners. In fact, as I said, I surmised he is the architect of their views of India. For you see, it was approximately forty years ago that he was in India. India at the time was a much poorer country than it is today. Technologically too, it was quite backward. Mercifully, today's India is materially far more affluent. Yet, the pastor cannot know that because he hasn't returned to India ever since his family and he came back to America. That was my tale of sojourn to the hinterlands of America. My spirits were deflated when we made it back to Seattle. What I had imagined the trip would be and how it turned out to be were drastically different. I had thought I would emerge triumphant and would have won over Allie's family. The place, the people were as interesting and as straight-of-Dickens as I imagined them to me. But, sadly for me, I cut a sorry figure among them. I was made to feel less than what I know I am. Allie sure is different. I do not know if it's because of the liberal education she received in a great American university or because of the substantial contacts she has come to have with foreigners lately, not to mention, yours truly. At any rate, she doesn't harbor the same less-than-human impressions of me. I am only glad.

Unfortunately, I am not able to write to you regularly. Since I folded this letter and now when I get back to it, six months have passed and a lot has happened. Allie and I are married! It all happened in a hurry. She, I, and a group of friends were taking a hike in a nearby National Forest area. As it happened, there was another couple that were part of the group. The guy had made elaborate plans to propose to the girl. I was privy to the plan. Allie was not. He had a diamond ring in his trouser pocket ready for the occasion. When we were casually hanging out in a picnic spot, he went on his knees and popped the age old question: "Will you marry me?" We knew they were deeply in love. Most of the time, you can expect the answer to this question to be a "yes". Otherwise, the guy wouldn't risk it. Behind the scenes, the couple would have negotiated for months about their marriage. Yet, to be fair, the day and the time for the question are kept under wraps. I have seen some of my friends (guys) deliberately punt on some good occasions to keep the slow boil in the girl's heart to keep going. Anyway, the girl on this occasion was genuinely stunned and burst into tears. It was heartwarming. Then they kissed, hugged, cried, and laughed. Love is a pure bliss. Allie, I, and the rest of the crew were only happy for them. What happened later was more spontaneous and even more impressive in my opinion. I am biased of course because as you know in a moment that I was a central character in that drama. While the proposal and the acceptance between that couple were taking place, Allie was casting a sideways glance at me. I understood that to mean she wanted a ring on her finger too! I haven't expressed it in so many words before, but Allie and I are deeply in love. I had been dreaming of marrying her and starting as a family for some months now. I was ready to pop the question on the spot. The only kink was, I didn't have a ring with me. I wear a ring that my mother has made me wear since when I was young. We had to keep refitting it to make it fit me as I went on getting bigger and bigger. It carries the blessings of Lord Hanuman. When Allie had seen me wear it on the ring finger, she had naturally assumed I was married. Later to soothe her nerves, she made me wear it on the index finger. The problem was solved—I had a ring with me after all. I reckoned it didn't have to fit perfectly for Allie. After all, this was a symbolic gesture.

I could always buy a new one for her any time when we are out of the woods, quite literally. When the newly engaged couple were finishing up their business, I went down on my knees and looked into Allie's beautiful face and with a bit of a trepidation, had a go at it. My instincts were not wrong. I will treasure the look of horror, surprise, and joy in Allie's face as long as I will breathe. She looked the happiest creature on earth at that moment. I was too because of her.

Her entire family except one brother joined us on the special occasion. My folks couldn't make it. Her folks are my folks too now. Allie and I lit the dance floor with our waltz. We had a month's long training to thank for it. I thought a new marriage calls for a new home too. I have bought a Single family home on the edge of a beautiful lake. That's where she and I have started our family life. It feels like paradise. I am enjoying the domestic bliss. Instead of coming home to my deserted flat after work, I come home to my home, our home. She is lovely. I like her face the best. Every time I see her, it feels like her rosy cheeks are beckoning me. She doesn't mind me showering her with kisses. Sometimes I feel she is my pet. She is much more than that of course. She is incredibly smart. She is well read. She is a double major in College: in Literature and Economics. She towers over me in those two subjects. She has a vast collection of books. We have designated a room as a library in our house. When she is not at work, she is in that library. I have gotten started with some of the classics she has recommended for me, Homer's odyssey to boot. She works as an Accountant in a reputed accounting firm. Her intellectual heft sometimes is intimidating. If I ask her a question, she makes a thorough job of answering it. I can't help but feel inadequate sometimes. I too know a thing or two about my craft: computers. I am trying to improve my elucidatory skills to match hers. What I find most disconcerting is, I cannot state and explain something as simply as she seems able to.

A marriage is a lot of adjusting also. I have to adjust to a new person and she has to to a new person. Something as mundane as where I like the newspaper to be kept needs rethinking and accommodation. I used to fling the Seattle Times that we get every morning on the sofa and I would let it lie there the whole day. Whenever I would slump on the sofa, I would glance over the pages and feel satisfied. Allie didn't like that. We bought a coffee table and she likes the newspaper to be kept in a tray on the underside of the coffee table whenever I am not reading it. I must say it led to a tiff between us. In fact, that was the first ever argument between us. My point to her was, "How does it matter?" Her point was, everything matters. I put together a string of what I thought were convincing arguments. She had an equally convincing case to make. Inter alia, she noted that when the newspaper is not read, it has no reason to be there. I had to concede that that was true. Additionally, she said, she doesn't read the newspaper. Therefore, the use of it was cut down to half in relation to the number of occupants of the house. That to me was the clincher. The truth of the statement was revelatory. It's not merely my house anymore. It's both of ours. I cannot possibly stamp around as though I am the only King. Now, there is an equally powerful and invested Queen as well. I have to confess that that simple statement changed my perspective. I at once softened. I have started looking at everything from both of our eyes as much as I am capable of. The question it comes down to is the following: "Are you prepared to share your life with the person you love?" The answer of course for pretty much everyone is, "Yes". If so, it then stands to reason that you behave in a way that makes sharing of life including your time, house, material belongings, feelings, misery, tribulations, joys, and friends possible. It takes a while to attain an equilibrium when two people come together. If both the parties are earnest in their love and in their desire to make the marriage work, then a harmonious equilibrium can be attained with some effort and in a reasonable amount of time. I am happy to report that she and I are both up for the challenge. Three months into the marriage, it feels like we have already achieved the marital bliss. I am glad I have her. I am sure she feels the same way about me too.

Expanding family, i.e., having a child sometimes crosses my mind. The marriage is in some sense a means to an end—the end being procreation. Allie and I have discussed it at length. She brings an intellectual viewpoint to the subject. She says, we should have a child exactly five years into the marriage. Why? She says by then you would have known your partner completely and if you have stayed together until then you would have concluded that you are meant for each other for life. That radical idea startled me. What is the marriage for then, if not for life? She is a progressive modern woman. She correctly says, I think, that she has seen too many marriages crumble before her eyes. If you make a baby and the marriage falls apart, that is not fair to the child. The child didn't come into the world expecting its parents to start living apart. Therefore, it's our moral obligation till the almighty time will bless our marriage with longevity, we shouldn't venture into the "start-the-family" business. When she explained it to me, I was literally stumped. However, I could see the wisdom of it. Even I can see that ephemeral infatuation, temporary successes have a lock on our emotions and we make judgments that we in the long run come to see as flawed. The old adage, "Only the time will tell" has a lot of truth packed into it. I am with her now. I too want to wait for five long or short years of gestation period and see if we can make a baby together for real. I fervently hope we do. In fact, I do not see how we won't be able to. She and I can't live apart even for a few days. When I go on business trips I miss her so sorely, so does she. When that is the case, us saying good-byes to each other permanently? Ah, you have got to be kidding me. I wouldn't be surprised if two years down the line, Allie comes around and says, "Two years have already told me what my intended five years would ever tell" and beg me to impregnate her. I am waiting for that day every day. But, what this enlightened thinking of hers has done is, it has put a full stop to any interminable discussions about making a baby. We don't have to talk about it every day. There could be a hidden perk too: we get to enjoy each other's company uninterrupted for five years. That's a good deal. Once a child or two are here with us, we won't be able to savor each other's company alone.

Hope you have settled down in your in-laws' place well. I am sure you will bring much joy and blessings to Amol and company. I am certain of it.

Love,
Akash

Chapter VI. Middle Class Travails

Dear Akash,

It has been ten years since I got married. Life is sprinting at a break-neck speed. How ardently I wish I could catch it and ask the question that bothers me everyday, "Why, me?" I have long lost a sense of direction in life. I do not see the point of anything that's happening to me. A life of happiness and comforts that I had foolishly imagined when I was yes, young and foolish turned out to be mere foolish thoughts after all. Amol and I have got two beautiful girls. They were nice until they were maybe 3–4 years old. The oldest is 8 and the youngest is 6 years old. It's a struggle just to dress them up for school, feed them enough food, and make them do the homework. They have grown more confrontational in the last few years. They bicker with each other incessantly. I have to act like a referee. When I go to resolve their fight, they gang up and start hurling abuses at me non-stop. They shout at the top of their voices that I am stupid, I am the worst mama that the world has ever seen, and that I am poor. The last insult I wholeheartedly admit to be true —I am poor, we are poor. What I cannot fathom is, where they might have learned to come up with such effective epithets for me. Amol lost his once secure government job when the government sold the insurance company he was working for to private shareholders. I am the sole bread-winner and bread-maker of our home. Amol's parents died in quick succession five years ago. His brother lives in a posh bungalow (more or less) in Delhi and his sister is married to a business tycoon (sort of) in Mumbai. Both have stopped visiting their poor brother for quite some time now. So, it's the four of us that make up our life. I would say, beyond the pecuniary concerns, we are doing fine. The saving grace is, Amol is as nice as ever and the bond between him and me is as strong as ever, and in fact myriad crises that we go through on a daily basis have brought us closer.

I am also fascinated by how the two children of mine harbor quite different personalities. They were born from the same womb and share the genes of the same father. But, they couldn't be more different. The oldest is a bit slow in school. The youngest is razor sharp in her intellect. Long ago, I stopped feeling that I understood them. They are altogether different persons. I can claim to understand them as much as I can claim to understand any kid at random I see on the streets. The other day I was just hunched and doing some back of the envelope calculations about our household expenses on a piece of paper. I hadn't even written any words. I was only scribbling numbers. My six year old approaches me and asks, "Is money a little tough right now, mama?" I was flabbergasted and my heart sank. I felt guilty that at this tender age that thought even crosses her mind. She has grown beyond her age to have a comprehension on the subject of finances. Anyway, she goes on to add that I won't have to get her a new dress for Diwali and that she will start drinking half a glass of milk instead of a full glass from now on to save money. Tears started rolling down my cheeks. She gave me a hug and giggled. I couldn't believe it. The oldest is a bit of a bossy kind. I don't know if it's uncouth to say that your child is selfish, but if I am being honest then I think I would certainly say so. She is as aware as the young one (or must be) of the precarious financial situation we are in, but her claims on privilege never cease. It's less about money and more about one's attitude. There was a trip organized by her teachers to go to Pune on a weekend. It was agreed that she would join the rest of her classmates on the trip. She wanted a new picnic bag, a new Summer dress, new sneakers, and a new water bottle! She had all of the accessories already, but for the trip the old possessions won't do. Her friend Kritika, ostensibly the daughter of a Tax Commissioner, is buying everything new. So, our kid who is born with a silver spoon also can't do without them.

Life is hectic, work is exhausting. There is not a moment's time for myself. Everyday I wake up at 5 AM. I don't have to set an alarm. I naturally wake up. The anxiety in me just makes me sit upright at that precise moment. Truth me be told, a lot of Mumbaikars do start cracking from 5. I guess, I am an average Mumbaikar. I take a quick bath and cook enough to last us through the night. I catch horrible local trains to get to work and reach the office by 9.30. I work at the Telephones department. Some days I have a lot more work than other days. The work per se is not overwhelming, but the very fact that I have to get to the office on good days and bad, and without a break makes me look and feel like a robot. I start back from the office at 5 PM and reach home by 6.30. The feeling of being home even though I experience it daily is heavenly. I wait eagerly for Amol to return. He is looking for work. So, sometimes he is out for longer hours. When he was working at the government insurance company, he used to be home before me and without fail, would bring me a hot cup of tea with copious amounts of ginger sprinkled in. All my worries and exhaustion would dissipate as soon as I would sip from that cup filled with Assam tea and Amol's love. He still does that if he is home. Then after a bit of sitting around, the running around starts. Some days, the older one does not want to hit the books, and some days the younger one. On those days when both are behaving well, it's the electricity that plays truant and cooking becomes a nightmare. If not that, a neighbor starts yelling at either me for my kids' ruckus, or he starts berating the other neighbor for not managing to stop their pet dog from barking. If the crown of the most discontented soul is to be awarded, my neighbor will beat the competition by miles. Our apartment is not big, but fortunately it does have two bedrooms. One for the girls, and one for the old couple. I feel good about it. So many people that I know and millions of people in Mumbai lack that privilege. If one room is all you have got then the entire family has to pile on top of each other, and the relationship between the husband and the wife, forget it. I know all that I am saying must be coming across as a most third world problem to you. You, who live in what you described as a mansion, should definitely wonder, "is such a life even a life?" Yeah, I agree. You need a certain amount of material wealth to live a decent life. Peace is another matter. We can't discount the role material wealth plays in one's overall well-being. That makes me think my family is a borderline case—I can't claim to be exactly poor and I can't claim to have enough either.

There is a lot of planning I am forced to do to cut down the expenses. I do not buy chopped vegetables. Instead I get whole vegetables and chop them on my own. Cut okra for example comes at the price of Rs. 50 for half a kilogram. If I buy it raw, then it is Rs. 28 for the same quantity. That makes a difference of Rs. 22 a day and a world of difference to us. From the saved money, I can purchase a notebook for Sneha (the first one) which will last her for three months and squeeze in a chocolate for Neha (the second one). Interestingly, the kids have started to help. At any rate, I am making them get started with chopping the vegetables, stirring the soup pot and such. If Amol is around, he is always an equal partner. No one makes daal like him. He is the best at it. The three of us savor his daal like it's Manna from heaven. The other big cost of our lives is the electricity bill. The government is intent on hiking the rates every year or so. I seriously wonder how all of my fellow citizens manage to foot the bills. I often think if it's only us who are being taken for a ride—many others just won't pay the bill, and the electricity board still generously keeps supplying them the marvel of modern life, and we hapless law-fearing people are made to cough up more money to compensate! I do not know. I have to surreptitiously undertake many actions to reduce the bill. At 2 AM when everyone is fast asleep and the breeze is cool, I turn off the whirring fans in the two rooms—my daughter's and ours. Nobody ever knows. Once Sneha asked how come when she got up the fan was turned off, and that she remembered it was on when she fell asleep. I did not answer lest she start insisting that it be kept on at all times. Of course, we reuse books and dresses of Sneha for Neha. Neha hasn't yet reached the age when she starts realizing what is being meted out to her. But, I am bracing for all hell to break loose when she stands up in revolt. I will have to sweeten the indignity somehow— shelling out money to buy her a new dress or something to compensate.

My father died five years ago. It was an unexpected, sudden demise. He had a cardiac arrest. I was devastated. Mom took it in her stride though. I was surprised. I had thought my mom would just crumble from the weight of the grief. She was affected, no doubt. But, she pulled herself up and became an example for my brother and me to emulate. My mother lives with my brother now. He got married two years after I did. I like my sister-in-law. She and I get along well. She is really nice. She doesn't harbor any malice, mal-intent. I am glad to see whenever I do see her. She is also glad to see me. It's really nice. There is a trope that two women cannot see eye to eye. We prove it wrong. In some way, I am proud of it too. I do not want to flatter myself, but I do think (quite gratuitously) that I am a reasonable, sensible woman, and without any significant vices. Most importantly though what I consciously, deliberately avoid is bad-mouthing others. Truth be told, humans of my sex do engage too much in that sort of behavior much to my consternation. I do not. I truly do not. Anyway, the point is, neither does my sister-in-law. We have never spoken about it to each other, but deep down in my heart, I feel I have found a kindred soul in her precisely for that reason. My mother and she also get along fine albeit with occasional disagreements. The disagreements that are inevitable when two people, be they mother-in-law and daughter-in-law, or husband and wife, not to mention mother and daughter live for an extended period of time together. But, my mother is also very sensible. So, never do their disputes escalate to the point that they cause rancor. As I alluded to it earlier, my husband's family is a different story. They are polar opposites of sense. They are utterly devoid of sense, and what's most disconcerting is, they equate money with status and success. First of all, I do not know why "status" is important. Second of all, even if we suppose it is, it needn't be equated with what car you have, how big your house is, or how much money is in your bank account. If I ever needed proof that such material barometers of success in life are baloney, I need not look further: they are living examples of how one can be moneyed and be carrying their bucket of wisdom empty. Did I just contradict myself? Oops. I was boasting that I do not badmouth anyone, but here I am—going on a diatribe against my own relations. In my defense, I would say this though: there is a fine line between stating things as they are, and seeing things in a poorer light for the heck of it.

I am always amazed by how equanimous Amol is through high points and low points. Sure, I must be biased in my opinion of him. I had better be biased being his wife. Yet, even when I examine his words, mind, and actions as dispassionately as I can, I can't help but marvel at how sound a mind he has got. His brother got married eleven months after we did. We were living as one big family then. His brother significantly hadn't become rich, arrogant, and an unwholesome man yet. The indications of the latter qualities were very much present though. His brother had just finished college and was looking for a stable job. He hadn't had the capacity to stand on his own feet yet. But, he charged ahead and got married to a girl who he had managed to woo at a local gym. That girl who comes from a lower middle class family and is one of seven siblings. She was just eager to get out of her overcrowded household. When he proposed to her, she quickly said "ok", and the marriage was solemnized in the next two months. It put enormous pressure on Amol and me to earn enough money to run the whole show because his parents being senior folks didn't have a great stream of steady income apart from the interest earned on their savings in the bank. What was most galling was, the couple lived like they were still college kids and without any regard for how their conduct would cause discomfort to others. The girl would wake up at 8 or 8.30 in the morning. She wouldn't cook, she wouldn't clean. It fell on me and my mother-in-law to cook for the big family. We put in the hard work. I had to rush to the office soon after we completed the morning chores. The brother's wife didn't have a job. She behaved as though she was on a holiday. She treated her in-laws house like a relaxing resort home. She would make all sorts of inappropriate comments too, like she would advise my mother-in-law to go on jogs because she would tell her openly that she is putting on a lot of weight. It was hard to tell if she was still immature or she just had the habit of making inane comments. For three years that I lived with her, I saw no remarkable hint of intelligence. God bless her and my brother-in-law. What was most annoying was, she would keep awake till 1.30–2 at night and watch TV at a very high volume. Even when we would tell her to keep it down, she would reduce the decibel levels for some time and its levels would come right back up just when we had fallen asleep again. That is where the equanimity of my husband comes into play. All the while when I was so distraught and complained nearly incessantly to Amol about the whole affair, he would tell me only one thing: how loving his brother was towards him and how close they were when they were young. That was his way of coping: I am sure he was as flabbergasted as everyone else, but he made a deliberate effort to focus on what was good about his brother so the whole situation looked tolerable.

I am worried about my children. I am constantly concerned how they will turn out to be when they are grown up. I was never destined for a life of glory. I do not necessarily want the girls to be queens of the world. But, what I do want for them is to have a better life than I did. First of all, the competition is just so intense everywhere—in schools and in the job market. Even so, I am not so deeply anxious about them not doing well in school or not finding a job. I believe they will do just fine on those fronts. What I am more worried about is, their personal lives. What kind of a guy would they would end up with, what kind of a family will they marry into are what cause me constant consternation. Because you see, these aspects are a function of pure luck. They are not in our hands. If you put in hard work, it's virtually guaranteed (provided you are endowed with enough intelligence by the all-powerful) that you will get good grades in school. What is not so certain is, if you look hard enough you will get a good guy. How many lives don't we see around us that are fully and completely wrecked because of the kind of partners the women and men in question chose? When I pray to God, I do not ask for wealth not for myself, not for my daughters. I pray for peace and happiness. It may sound quaint and maudlin, but hey, I know enough now to grasp what matters in life. If it had not been for Amol, my life even in sounder financial conditions, would have been an absolute misery. What trumps the love of your husband and his steady hands to guide you and give you company in this erratic world? In one word—nothing. When Sneha and Neha grow up what I hope they will remember from this difficult period of our lives is not so much how much we suffered because we were not rich, but that we were a family, a close-knit loving family where their mother and father loved them unconditionally and that we did the best we could for them.

I am eager to hear how your marriage
probation period progressed. I am certain you
passed it with flying colors and you and Allie
are proud parents to princes and princesses.

Love,
Saroja

Chapter VII. Middle Age Crisis

Dear Saroja,

Before I know it I have turned 45. I am glad I still have a good old friend to reminisce of old ways and old times. If I live up to 90 and it doesn't appear I will be able to push past that figure, I have certainly reached my middle age. Life spent growing up with you half a world away seems to be from another lifetime. Life as I knew it is no more. I have everything and I have nothing. I have lost my identity. I am a changed man. I know I don't like what I see of myself in the mirror. Crucially I do not know how to fix it either. I have given up on myself and I have given up on life.

Allie and I broke up two and a half years into our marriage. Looking back, that was the most stable period of my life. I guess frustrations were building up inside of me and her the whole time and finally, an innocuous looking dispute just ended our fledgling marriage completely. I do not hate her. I don't even know where she is or what she is up to. Divorcing is a matter of a couple of days' of simple paperwork in America. It takes nothing to just bid each other goodbyes and move on in opposite directions. There were no families of hers or mine involved when we were married and nobody was there to see if things could be mended between us. It was a swift and a silent affair, the parting of us that is. One fine morning she offered to make Chicken tikka masala for me. I said that I was a vegetarian and couldn't partake in the delicacy she was offering to make. She instantly grew furious and said she had been researching it for the past two days, watched innumerable YouTube videos on it, and after all that she asked how I could refuse when she so lovingly wanted to make it for me? I told her she knew for long I did not eat meat and even then how she could insist that I eat Chicken. I was perplexed. Seriously, how could she not have known and how could she insist? She didn't answer the question. But, I suspect it slipped out of her mind that Chicken is meat after all. In any case, she just threw up her hands and said she didn't believe she was living with a jerk like me all that while. I was flabbergasted. I gave her back as good as I got. She promptly moved out to live in a hotel the same instant. She hauled her personal stuff two days later to an apartment she said she had found somewhere. The very next month we were in a courtroom dissolving our marriage. In the haze of things I couldn't fathom why it had happened. Much later I could put a finger on where things had started to go awry. It was simply that we were much too incompatible. Our cultural differences were just too vast which we couldn't bridge with our real love and the best of intentions. Her and my friend circles hardly overlapped. When I was in the company of her and her friends, I just couldn't get the jokes they were cracking and howling with laughter as though a most potent joke bomb had detonated. They had a lot of cultural landmarks that they used as their guide posts in their conversations. They talked of the sitcoms they had watched growing up. They were deeply familiar with the Hollywood movie stars, and their personal lives. I hardly had an interest in those matters. So, I remained a through and through outsider in their circle. I didn't have much of a friends circle of mine to boast of. Of the friends that I had, most of them and in fact all of them had been Indian immigrants like me. She and I would join with them for Diwali parties and the like sometimes. When we used to light up lamps and put Rangolis on, or sing some Bollywood songs together, Allie was genuinely interested. But, being not deeply cognizant of the stories and the rationale behind our myriad customs myself, I was answerless to her curious and probing questions. She used to feel disappointed when I couldn't explain the God's praise I used to sing in Sanskrit to her. All in all, it was a case study in how a long term marriage cannot come to stand if the partners do not share something deep. Share we didn't.

From then on I was a drifter. My professional life was fulfilling and made steady progress. In fact, having nothing to look forward to in my personal life, I dedicated more energy and time into work. It became my raison d'être. I achieved a higher title after a higher title. I was making millions of dollars a year. It struck me as somewhat interesting that the top bosses of the company that I had become pals with had no moral compass. I took inspiration from them. Many of them were married and had kids. But, they hardly spent much time at home. They would either be at office or at restaurants cajoling the clients, or on the road. I got to see them up close. Soon I started realizing that the men (most of them were men) almost always had girlfriends. The girlfriends would travel with them on their business trips. The men were middle aged. The girls were always young. The cast of girlfriends would keep changing. Nobody talked of them, nobody questioned the powerful men. It was just a given fact that they would have female company wherever they went—be it office parties, trips, or restaurants. The men had a cavalier attitude towards everything—they would dismiss the clients in private, they had no reverence for the company that we were working for, and of course they didn't care a damn about the girls they slept with. One day, a top executive came back from a vacation and in the middle of a business meeting blurted out something honest. He was clearly moved. He said in the prior five days he had spent with his family, he realized that his children had grown up. He had three kids. He had a lump in his throat when he said he was startled to discover that they had developed unique personalities of their own. When he reaches home at 10 PM or so on every week day, the children would have gone to bed and in the morning when he rushes out of the home at 8 AM, they are busy getting ready for school. So, he hadn't had a chance to have meaningful interactions with them for years. On weekends, he heads out to play golf with the C.E.O or some other powerful men and hence on weekends too he had no time to spend with his wife and kids. It was a moving spectacle. For a change, I got to glimpse the real souls of the executives who I call my company. Despite the façade of "having it all" and the toughness that these folks betray, just below the surface, they are really hollow and are totally miserable people. Yet, I couldn't help but imitate them. I became one of them. I didn't have a family to boot. I didn't make an effort to build one either. All these years later, here I am—a middle aged, morally bankrupt sad man.

I had fun all these years. To be truthful, while I was indulging in it, I did feel I was having fun. The fun was always ephemeral and once it was over, I felt as empty as ever. To cover up the true emptiness of my life, I craved for more "fun". More fun came and went, yet I was left with where I was before or worse. Once I had acquired money, it was not very difficult to find girls or friends to spend time with. I would sponsor their trips to Las Vegas. We would fly down to Legas for weekends, have plenty of sex, booze as much as we wanted, and sink as much money as we wanted in the slot machines. Invariably after a few months, the girls that I used to hang out with would find more stable relationships and leave my side. I didn't use to feel very sad because I would never be emotionally attached to them. However, their leaving would necessitate finding a new girl and training them for my needs. One time I was truly attracted to a girl. Her name was Linda. There was something special about her. I could sense it from the beginning. Soon I discovered she was very well read. Strangely she reminded me of Allie. Like Allie, Linda too was a bookworm. She had read many English classics. Her talk was intelligent. I was hooked. Being with her, I could at once realize what I was sorely missing in life: meaningful conversations about life, intellectually, emotionally gratifying debates to make sense of seeming arbitrariness of life. She and I talked. Seeing my sorry state— inebriation, use of foul language soon convinced her however what a pathetic creature I was. She lasted for less time than on average how long other girls had lasted. I recently ran into her at a business party. She was with her beautiful husband. She had become a hotshot herself at a startup. This is what you can do with talent—rise up through the career ladder. If you have the awareness about life too, then you can build a family as well. I probably had some worldly talent. I only stopped at it. I don't think I didn't have the capacity to have the foresight to strive for what is truly important in life in the long-term: having strong relationships with other people, doing good for others. It's simply that I became intellectually lazy and deliberately chose not to see that aspect of life.

How did I arrive at all these realizations now seemingly all of a sudden? Well, you never do until something calamitous happens in life. That is to say, something calamitous has happened in my life. Life has come to a screeching halt. The Porsche I was driving has crashed and is a wreck of its former self. My car is a perfect metaphor for my life too. I lost my job. In the creative destruction of a capitalist society, it's inevitable that some people lose their jobs at random intervals while others build fortunes. I was more sad than shocked. I have been at it long enough to know that the axe could very well fall on me some day. The intellectual preparation notwithstanding, when you have plenty of time in your hands and have no idea what to do with it, it can be pretty disconcerting. I had built a house, and had amassed enough savings to tide over the bottom of a career I was navigating. The problem was, I had nobody to spend the extra time with it. So I hit the strip clubs, and bars. Once when I was returning from a bar after mild intoxication, I hit the divider on the freeway and sent my life into a tailspin. It happened six months ago. I was taken to a hospital. The doctors found that my spine was broken and my right femur bone had splintered. I was in the hospital for two months. The time in the hospital was a haze. I was too decimated to have a clear mind. Things were happening to me rather than I was making things happen. Once I came back home, I started coming to my senses. I started realizing what a mess of a life I had made for myself. The physical pain and rehabilitation in some sense were the easy part. I started crying. I don't even remember when I had cried last. But, the emotional toll my twenty years of life in America had extracted was finally bursting forth. My parents are long dead. I have no real contacts with my relatives in India. I had stopped writing to you too. I was living the American dream. I had become convinced that I was shooting for the pinnacle of success and that I was really getting there. When I used to see my Indian friends devoting their evenings and weekends to ferrying their kids to hockey matches and piano classes and such I used to think they were great morons. I, in my Porsche used to drive to golf courses, hobnob with other bastards who nevertheless were powerful. However, in the recent months when I was alone at home confined to my bed most of the time having no energy or strength to engage in any activity, all I could think of was my childhood home and my mom and dad. I don't know where those memories were buried all this time. Without prompting, my mind would only go back to these memories. It's as if that's the only thing that has happened in my life. I even remembered a bad dream I had when I was barely four. I must have woken up crying and when I had opened my eyes, I was in my mother's lap. I heard her say—"He must have had a bad dream". I had slowly drifted back to sleep. I wanted to reach out to my mother and father. I wanted my mother by my side as I writhed in pain. I wanted my father to bring me my medicine. Well, there was no father, no mother. Heck, there was no wife or kids too that I very well could have gained in their stead. Now I do think that life is not to be taken lightly. One has to be strategic. I know I am sounding mercantilist when I am saying this, but it's from the point of view of one's soul. You have to sacrifice something (like a bit of a career success) to earn peace in life (a family). You can't have both. Probably you can have both too—if you invest in both and are lucky. As time passes by, the little career success I had, is losing its meaning. I have ten million dollars in my bank account today. What good comes of it when it's useless to find a good, virtuous wife or a close friend? There are two successes to aim for in life: material and spiritual. My material coffers are seemingly in good shape while the spiritual affairs are bankrupt.

The acts that used to make me incredibly happy when I was young had ceased to satisfy me to the same extent in the last couple of years even before the car accident. I used to feel dizzy with esoteric excitement when I used to stay awake with my girlfriend the whole night. It had started looking banal. How many times can you go to Vegas anyway before it loses its allure? Golf still was interesting. I could engage in some physical exercise while not exerting myself too much. The men I used to hang out with were coming across as boring. It's the same talk *always*—some innuendos about female executives, boasting about their recent escapades, and trash talking one another. I had started wondering if these men have no refined tastes. It seemed to me that their intellectual growth had hit a dead-end. Never once did I see them discuss an interesting book they had read or any book for that matter, or a new insight they had gleaned while being with their kids. "Is this all?" was the running refrain I used to feel. I had started feeling like a robot. To fit in, to hold onto the position I had as the Marketing Head of the company, I had to or I thought I was expected to anyway to use foul language at work—ridiculing the clients, asking my reports how their families were even though I had not an iota of interest in the matter, fawning over my bosses, and losing deliberately to them on the golf courses. "Me" was lost in my acts. It increasingly felt like I had no freedom for self-expression and no voice left that I could say was authentically my own. I didn't even know who my authentic self was.

In a way I think when I crashed my car on a freeway it must have come as a blessing in disguise. If I had sustained a minor injury, then I would have felt the need to get back onto the hamster wheel right away. But, a major injury like the one I got gave me the time to recuperate not only my body but also my soul. At least I now know what I was doing. What I should do next is still unclear. A part of me wants to pack up and return to India. A part of me wants to go back to life as it was albeit hopefully with a better self of me. I am genuinely torn. I had been to Mumbai last year to meet my sister and her family. My niece is all grown up. I had met them after a gap of five years. India had changed, they had changed, and I felt it was only me who hadn't. When I went to see them I had expected things to be pretty much as they were when I had visited them last. Well, it appears it's only me who refuses to grow up. They had a bigger house and were doing well. My niece who I was good friends with had become a college girl. As kids grow, they become different kids each year. So, of course I shouldn't have expected to see the same talkative, naughty girl when I saw her. I couldn't help but lament that I hadn't built a family. Seeing my sister's family made me acutely aware of what I was losing in my life—as my own life invariably hurtles towards the end, I had not created half-replicas of me roaming on earth to carry forward what my personality was made up of, for what it was worth. I felt utterly alone seeing my folks. As I ponder on the matter at this time if I should return to India, I experience the trepidation of having to start all over again—a new house, new environs, the heat, the hustle-bustle, and sorry the filth too of India. Sometimes I think my idea of returning to my homeland is just a romantic thought for me. Probably I can never bring myself to return to India and I am maybe

destined to be here. I am gaining my strength.
I don't think I can sit at home much longer. The
last half year has been a semi-retirement for
me. I think I have another sprint to run before I
can take a permanent retirement.

Love,
Akash

Chapter VIII. Into retirement

Dear Akash,

I hadn't expected that we would be pen pals as long as we have been. I retired from work last week. I had turned 60 a couple of months ago. In India, in most jobs if you are lucky you would be sent home packing to a life of retirement when you hit that pre-designated age. I still am fine. I still am as capable as in my 40s, but sure, I will take a life of retirement when I am still healthy and when I still have strength in my legs and hands to enjoy a few years before I am really forced to retire from life. When I got a break from the frenetic pace of life to contemplate on life that has been thus far, I couldn't but think that I really have lived many lives in a single life of mine. When I look back at my younger self, I can't help but marvel at how wise I was even then. Well, I cannot speak for now but I can certainly say I was then. I do not feel abashed when I praise my younger self because when I am talking of her, I feel I am talking of a different person and it's really not me who I am praising. I feel quite distinct from her. It was a different person who supposedly I was at one time. I am grateful to her for what she did for without her hard work and sacrifices I couldn't be where I am today. I can with much thanks in my heart say, I am in a place of comfort and peace.

Life did not exactly turn out how I had imagined it to be much less how I dreamed it to be. But, I will happily take what I got eventually. There were many ups and downs like we can expect there to be in anyone's life. The downs were never too crushing and the ups were never as numerous as I would have liked them to be. The girls are grown up. The oldest—Sneha is married and the youngest—Neha is still with us biding her time to attain escape velocity to break out of our gravitational force to become an independent star. While I was writing this I realized I will not and cannot write—"Sneha is married off" for who are we to marry her off? At any rate, she found herself a good beau and we were there to officiate the ceremonies. The two girls were quite autonomous. They made all big decisions for themselves. We were not called upon and we couldn't anyway, make those decisions for them—be it what they wanted to study, which college to enroll into, what friends to make, with whom to hang out with, and in the case of the oldest which guy to marry, and in the case of the youngest too—who to marry in the future. They were quite sensible in their choices. They were not intellectual superstars of their times, but I am glad to say, they had enough common sense in them to not ruin their lives irreparably.

The money matters eased quite a bit after I had written of our precarious pecuniary situation last time. I got a promotion and Amol got a job. After the new pay commission constituted by the Central Government recommended a 20% salary hike across the board, we were more or less swimming in money. Things went on fine for many years. When a life of tranquility and monotony had descended on us, fate decided to throw a curveball to mix things up a bit. Amol's sister's husband died unexpectedly. Our relationships with his brother and especially with his sister had thawed quite a lot. After his sister had a son and when it appeared that that son is heading straight for a life of F's as far as the academics were concerned, she mentally came down from her pedestal and started to appreciate common sense where it existed. She did see grounded-ness in us and our girls. She would visit us once in a while and was being nice to Sneha and Neha. She would from time to time seek my advice on matters such as what strategy to adopt towards her son to make him study and when she thought her husband was going off the rails in his business decisions, she would invite Amol and me home and have us counsel him. He was not a bad fellow. He was in a bad company though. As far we knew, he was doting towards his wife and son. But the problem was, he had taken to gambling. We do not know the exact details but it involved games of cards. He would spend a few hours a night in some underground pub and engage in that activity. He was not a drunkard but he would gulp down quite a few pegs often enough. He didn't die of liver failure however, which I was most concerned about. He died of a cardiac arrest. He was lanky—lean and tall. I do not know how his heart gave way, but give way it did. Thankfully, he was not in deep debt or anything of the sort. After he passed away, Amol helped his sister find a footing. He helped her chase down his finances. As you can expect, the financial arrangements were quite murky for he was a shrewd businessman. It took a good amount of head scratching and running from pillar to post to retrieve the money hidden behind an opaque web of linkages. But, in the end, there was enough for her and the son to live a life of moderate comforts and do well in life, if they chose to. For the most part, they did. The son seemed chastened from the experience and slowly came back on track. He grew up. He is of a similar age as Neha. He graduated with a degree in Commerce and is setting up a business of his own. I am beginning to admire him. He comes across as a sensible fellow. But, when his father died, Amol was stricken. For one, blood is thicker than water. Whatever the past bitter experiences were, he was worried to death for his sister. When he so unexpectedly died, it was not clear what his financial condition was. Our worry was, he had left behind a mountain of debt. Thankfully, that turned out to be not the case. It took nearly a year to sort out the mess. When we were in the clear, life returned to a semblance of normalcy for Amol and me.

Neha flunked in her tenth grade exams. She failed in English of all the subjects. She speaks English OK, in fact better than average. To pass and to earn good marks on the English exam you can't just show off your English prowess. You must have studied the chapters that are on the syllabus. I do not know how her struggle with English had slipped out of my radar too. After the results were announced I asked her if she had read the English textbook. Her answer was she didn't recall. I was aghast. In the zeal to make sure she did well in mathematics, social sciences, and science which she had declared as tough subjects for her, we had completely neglected English. It was tough. I was demoralized. When her friends' mothers were excitedly discussing what college to send their kids to for 11th and 12th grades, life had stopped for me. Well, it must have been tougher for Neha more than for the rest of us. She took it with aplomb I must say. As usual our saint Amol didn't lose his head. When none of us were up to cooking food or eating, he cooked for us and fed us too for the most part. It was during the depths of that winter—for Neha didn't pass the supplementary exam too and lost a whole year, that I started feeling that there was a higher power after all. When nothing seems to be in your control, you start to ask the question "Who is?". It was the period of my spiritual awakening. To the extent that I am awakened today, it can be traced back to that period of helplessness and utter despair. I occasionally listened to great evangelical orators of yore and our times of all faiths. But, it's not so much what I listened to but what I thought to myself that started convincing me that everything is preordained. It started looking as though there ought to be a purpose behind everything. Every success and particularly every failure conceals behind it a great deal of purpose, a purpose that we cannot yet see but sure enough will manifest itself in time. We only have to wait. Looking back, that episode of failure brought forth two changes: one, I became a far more peaceful person internally and Neha rose up from the ashes like a phoenix from that sordid episode.

If those are some of the lows of my life, the highs too came at a fitful frequency. It's who Sneha befriended and married that has warmed my heart the most. His name is Mayur. He came across as a sensible fellow from the start. They have a four year old son now. It's seeing him becoming the pampering father that has convinced me more than anything else that Sneha made the right choice. You can love a man or a woman for a myriad of reasons: their intellect, beauty, money, or for no reason at all. If that love endures and carries over to the next generation you created together, that's when I believe the timelessness of love shines more. He is quite egalitarian. He, unlike most other fathers, takes a lot of responsibility for bringing up my grandson. I am quite happy for Sneha. If Amol was the best thing that happened to me, I would venture so far as to say Sneha is, if anything, luckier. Truth be told, Mayur is a notch more intelligent than Amol. For all his good heart, Amol is a bit lacking in the intellectual department. I do not see any glaring flaw in Mayur in contrast. I hear from Sneha that he can be a disciplinarian at times. Maybe that is his flaw. I have to take her word for it because if he indeed is a stickler in matters of his living, he has done a tremendously good job of concealing it from us thus far. Incidentally, that has upped the expectation for Neha—she wants a husband no less capable than Mayur. I sometimes think that has delayed her finding a beau for herself. She doesn't want to come up short relative to her big sister. When Mayur and company with their little fellow do visit us, our house is full and our hearts are warm. A feeling of thorough contentedness envelopes the entire household.

Despite having been surrounded by a loving family, I have to admit that at times I have felt utterly lonely intermittently in the past several years and decades. The cares of life had worn me down. Amol though was always there, the spark of love was barely alive between us. Deep depression was the result. I didn't seek psychotherapy. The awareness of what it was I was feeling was low plus to boot there was no money or time to seek it. Those were the darkest days of my life. The darkest period lasted for maybe around two years. Melancholy descended on me without warning one fine morning when I woke up. I had thought I was only feeling a bit low that day as it had happened several times before. I was baffled because when the days dragged on, I couldn't pinpoint what it was that was causing me such utter despair. Cause despair it did. There were several reasons to be unhappy about. Sneha was just starting high school and Neha was just finishing up middle school. I felt like a cog in the wheels of their lives. I had to cook, clean, earn, and take abuses from them for advising them to not ruin their lives—by asking them to do their homework, and to cultivate good friendships. I couldn't see what the point of my existence was. "I" was lost. It appeared that the days of hard work and hardship appeared endless. Years had gone by and more years would roll by when I would still be engaged in the monotonous ways of holding us above water. There hardly was free time to sit and relax for myself or to visit a new place I hadn't been to or had someone to hold my hands and ask, how I was doing or what I was feeling. I wanted to return to a simpler life, a life of my youth when the dreams were still alive and the future was still ahead of me. I felt then that there really was no special purpose to our lives, at any rate, to my life especially. We just have to do our bit to pass the torch from our ancestors to the next generation. I still believe that. Dawning of that eternal truth can be disconcerting. When we start out in life mainly when we have sufficiently developed our wings and are about to explore the world on our own, we harbor romantic notions about life. We tend to think we are special, we will make our lives unique and special in some way. For me it was the belief that my love for Amol was greater than any love the humankind had ever seen before. Our love story was my burning ambition. The tender emotions I felt for him gave me a greater purpose. With time when that higher calling that I had told myself existed dissipated, I felt lost. I began to feel, I am no better or no more distinguished than millions of other people around me. There was nothing remarkable about me or my life. It's true. I even today do not know how to overcome that firm conviction. In a calm analysis of our lives, I believe there is no escaping that logical conclusion which we reach, if we take the trouble to think of life and our living in the context of eternity of time and life. Yet, we have to live on, we have to do our part. At some point, we have to make peace with that inescapable reality of our beings. I do not know if I truly made peace with that realization or not, but carry on I did. Or, perhaps equally appropriately, life and time just carried me forward. Here I am today, after a significant unburdening of my responsibilities, sitting and feeling good again about my life. It's my daughters who have to carry forward that burden from here on. The baton has been passed. I know that no amount of my advising them of my life's lessons will bring them succour in their own lives. They have to go through the crucible of life themselves, have to experience the ups and downs life will invariably throw at them, and have to come away through it onto the other side as much unscathed as possible.

The other day when Sneha, Mayur and the little prince had come to our place and were readying to return to their home, what transpired was emblematic of life. Sneha was repacking the bag to get ready to leave. The little fellow had a bathroom emergency. His mother hadn't got extra clothes. She became exasperated and started yelling at the boy. After much scrambling about, we got hold of an old dress of Amol, cut it into the right size and made it fit on him. When he emerged smug faced from the dressing room to present himself to the wider audience, the glee and laughter on everyone's face was irrepressible. Sneha too was all smiles. When she had started shouting at the innocent life, I wanted to grab her and shake her out of her wrong notions of life. I wanted to tell her, life will never progress the way she plans much less how she dreams. Making plans certainly is in her hands and is her prerogative, but how the events will unfold is not. So, she had better internalize that lesson right then and there. I didn't drill down that lesson in her though. I kept quiet holding to myself the pain of witnessing how deeply unfair she was being to the little boy and equally, how much more she had yet to learn to grow up. I do not know when everything was finally in order, if she had the chance to think of the incident in the broader metaphorical terms that I am describing it to you now, but I only hope she did. If not, she had better assess it in the larger-than-life terms soon.

My kids have organized a retirement party for me next month. I am not feeling the exasperation that people say you encounter when you retire. For one, I did not hold a big post and am not retiring from being an all-important person to being a nobody. For another, I guess I was mentally prepared. As a matter of fact, I was looking forward to what I hope will be tranquil years of my life. The kids have bought Amol and me plane tickets to fly to the Maldives. We will spend a week there on the beaches soaking in the sun. It's ironic. Always through our youthful years we were cash strapped. In my advanced years, I am getting to enjoy my honeymoon. Why not? It's better than the alternative—if I was well off when I was young and poor when I am old. That I suppose would be worse. I will gladly take it. I am feeling like a new bride again. I am exuding a newfound love for Amol. I think I will blush like a new bride when we embark on that plane journey to join the honeymooners and beachgoers in the Maldives.

I trust you recuperated from your car crash well. It has been quite a while I have heard from you. Do let me know what you are discovering in your life.

Love,
Saroja

Chapter IX. After a long pause

Dear Akash,

I recently came across the term—platinum jubilee. I have heard that word on and off my entire life but it had never completely registered in my mind how many years that it was supposed to stand for. However, I do not think I will forget from now on exactly how many years a platinum jubilee is to mark. It is 75 years of course. You and I will both be celebrating our platinum jubilees! I think we are at right around the point when statistically speaking, we are to fade into oblivion. I being in India is likely to die sooner than you who in America are expected to live longer. I haven't heard from you for close to thirty years. But having known your mind when we both could barely walk and talk, I am sure you do not mind this intrusion from me from your native land.

Amol died five years ago. He was a young fella. He never lost his boyish face and his youthful manners. He succumbed to the new plague that's devouring men across the world—heart attack. It's actually a lot worse than other diseases. With other diseases like that of lungs or kidneys where you get quite a bit of forewarning about the future you are to face without your loved ones, the sudden stopping of the heart stops the heartbeats of more than one person—of the one one who is dead certainly and of the ones who are left behind. Amol and I were having absolutely a blast of life when the Goddess of death hauled him away in his sleep at the dawn of a morning. It was a little unusual for him to have not woken up at his usual 6 O'clock in the morning on the fateful day. I got up at 7 and saw that he had turned the other way facing away from me. He had his hand clutched to his chest and seemed to still be in deep sleep. I did not want to wake him up for I thought it may have been some kind of an exhaustion of the previous day and he was sleeping it out. So I left him alone or so I thought anyway at the time, and went about my business in the kitchen and the rest of the house. I called out for him from the living room at around 8 O'clock exhorting him to come out to read his favorite newspaper—The Times of India. For the love of my life, I could never figure out what was so interesting spending hours together with your head buried in the same old goings on of the world. Clearly, he felt there was something new and interesting about it everyday because that is how he spent and I always believed wasted, precious 1.5 hours of his mornings each day. That morning though, he did not answer my irresistible call to read his newspaper. Panic struck me like lightning. I knew something was terribly wrong. Suddenly I realized even without entering the bedroom what his hand-on-the-chest pose meant. When the paramedics came, they pinpointed his time of death to be 5.30 AM. I hear that the crack of dawn is the time for cardiac arrests. I cannot say I heard a murmur at the time. Maybe I was dreaming sweet dreams or nightmares in my sleep. I do not remember. Regardless, a real nightmare was taking place in my waking world at that precise time.

It has been a hard climb since then. It's akin to recovering from a broken bone. I could finally relate to what you were describing about your horror of broken spine and femur bone after getting into a car crash. I had had a mental crash. Each day was a slog. Being a naturally alert person, I had no trouble getting out of bed, and taking care of life's cares and chores before. After Amol's death however, I felt a sense of paralysis. I found it hard to even physically move. I realized the connection between the body and the mind. Your stress, your grief will cause physical pain to you. It was astounding to watch how it was true with myself. I had been quite chatty and I had a large friends' circle. I was the Secretary of the ladies' club in our society. I was a constant fixture there most evenings. Light gossiping with old and young ladies would give me pleasure. Now, it was gone. I couldn't find the slightest amusement or comfort in my old habits. I am not sure what it was that I was mourning—loss of Amol, or a loss of purpose in life, or a loss of love, or a loss of security in life. It's hard to put a finger on it. All I knew was that I couldn't go on. If my daughters asked me as to why, I did not have a coherent answer either. Like with a fractured bone, you don't heal overnight. It's not a switch that goes on your mind and you wake up from your grieving slumber. Healing is gradual. Months and years must roll by before you start feeling like your previous self. That is what happened to me. With five years interposed between Amol's death and now, I can breathe slightly easily, strike a conversation with fellow human beings amicably, and again think of the pleasures life has to offer. I am happy to write that I have recovered.

That brings me to the chief purpose of writing to you at this time. I have been thinking you could move to Mumbai again. I have run the idea through the girls. They are more than happy to have you here. We will find a comfortable house for you and help you settle down. I do not know what your personal circumstances are at present. But my heart tells me you are alone. If so, why not move back? I have no company and assuming you have no company, we can be company to each other. Even though we haven't seen each other in person for more than fifty years now, I suspect we are still cosmically connected. Our relationship has always been platonic. At this late stage in our lives it cannot be anything else. We naturally open up to each other and think of the other as an extension of our own selves. I see a lot of advantages to your making Mumbai your home again. Not least in my mind is the consideration and even the exuberance that I can talk to you, spend time with you, reminisce our old days of childhood again. Truth be told, I am ecstatic at the prospect of having you close by. I do not think you have visited India often after you left Mumbai for good in your early 20's. India of today is quite different from the one you left behind. I have not seen America, so I cannot readily compare how India fares in relation to it. However, seeing

India change before my own eyes, I can unequivocally tell you, it's more prosperous, it's more progressive, and it's more comfortable. What's more, my daughters will be your daughters. My grandchildren will be your grandchildren. The last thing I want in the world is for you to die there alone. Know that you have a family in us. We are eagerly waiting to hear affirmatively from you on this proposal.

By the way, Neha got married after I had written to you last. We found a nice chap for her. They are happily settled in Delhi. The oldest grandson from Sneha just finished his tenth grade and is in eleventh grade now. My days mostly pass in idleness. I have taken up reading in a big way. I had not been much of a reader throughout my life. I accidentally picked up "Autobiography of a Yogi" and I was hooked. I was hooked to that book and all the books that were to follow. It was not so accidental that I stumbled upon the Yogi book: sometime after Amol left us, Neha's husband had presented it to me and had urged me to read it. It was supposed to be a spiritual book and he had thought that the book may bring me some solace. Solace it did bring and more. I became a fan of books. Every day I have the anxious sense that I am waging a losing battle—the eyes, I expect will begin to fail me any moment now and I have barely scratched the surface of the literary world. Yet, I am satisfied. I will die knowing that I read at least a few gems of what men and women of all of humanity of the present and the past had to offer me. I wonder at times why I didn't discover the joy of reading before. Yet, I am not too terribly repentant about it. Reading can be taxing. I invariably get entangled in the drama of the characters the authors create for me. I partake in their tribulations and feel exuberant in their accomplishments. But, the authors being clever from life experiences have me participate in their creations' sufferings more often than their joys. On the whole, when I am done with my reading at the end of the day, I feel tired, tired mentally. Physically I am supposed to be tired anyway at my age.

After my own little tryst with books I am ruminating with fascination what books represent and how they are magic embodied in written pages. Books can be a great equalizer. It does not matter if I am sitting in India or America if I have in my hands a great book. Similarly, it does not necessarily matter if I am poor or rich, or if I was educated in a good school or in a mediocre one. For when I have access to a book and have the capacity to read and understand it, I have an equal chance at new education and new enlightenment as anyone else in the world. I find that thought truly marvelous. I recently bust a misconception regarding books that I used to harbor myself. Prior to the realization that I am going to relate, I used to feel that one should read "classics" and not waste time on other newbies in the block. I am all for judging a book's literary merit. There indeed are many books that are written poorly. Yet, one shouldn't be too fastidious about the stature of the author or have prejudge a new gem of an insight a book has to offer. And, here is why: each book, we have to realize, is a mirror to the times of its writing. The author necessarily is channeling the cultural milieu of his/her times. So, a book quite apart from its literary merit serves another purpose—to hold a mirror to the society of the time. Every book is a book of history too. When people say, "Oh, I have nothing new to say that has not been said before" when they are asked if they considered writing a book themselves, they couldn't be more wrong. Even if we write their own autobiographies, that will be a tremendous service to the future generations of humankind because they will learn how we lived, the technologies we used, how we behaved with one another, and what our beliefs were. I would be curious to learn the ways of living five hundred years ago from a person who lived at the time. A person spaced similarly into the future, I am sure, would be equally interested to learn of the aspects of life of a current person.

Having your life partner taken away is an irreparable loss. Although I am lucky that I have kids and grandkids and they are well disposed to me, it still is a lonely existence. When Amol was living, I had a companion every step of the way. We would wake up together, eat together, go out together and sleep together. He was a constant presence. Now, I am alone. We had a long shared life too. His children were my children and mine his. There was so much of "our" in our lives. There were just so many shared life experiences. We had close to fifty years of life absolutely with another. Now I feel I am living both of our lives. I am living my life for him for he missed the extra years I am going to spend on earth. Not a moment goes by when I don't think of him. He is always there. One who hasn't lost a spouse cannot fully comprehend the lives we as windows or widowers lead, I think. My daughters have moved on as they rightly should. Papa for them is somewhat of a removed figure now. They feel that they did what they could for him when he lived and are performing their duties towards me to the best of their abilities. It is enough for them. I totally support their view. But, I wish I could say the same about me. I cannot. His presence was required more for my own sake. Long ago, my daughters had become the "givers" for him and he had become the "taker". For me, he was always a "giver". In fact, there was no giver and taker between us. We were both givers and takers when it came to the relationship between us. It's as though a half of me is dead and I am straggling behind him with the other half. I do not know if there is an afterlife or not, but how ardently I wish sometimes I join him wherever he is.

The changing social mores astound me. It's a different India compared to when you and I grew up. It's more liberal. What that means is, sexual relations and romantic relations are to be found in more abundance and we can be sure to see them dissolve at rates that were unimaginable when I was a young belle. A guy or a girl today would have had on average 2–3 girlfriends or boyfriends before they find their spouse. When they find a spouse also, surely that doesn't mean the end of the story. The marriage can break any time. Hope you do not mind me saying it, it then cannot be termed a marriage. If you are not sure you are going to be with that person for the rest of your life, then why marry at all? You should continue to live in a live-in relationship until you are sure you will be together till death does you apart and then marry. Or, if you cannot ever be sure then don't marry at all. I give you an extra benefit of the doubt because you married an American woman. Therefore, you are excused from the stringent marriage line I am drawing. When I attend weddings I have stopped feeling the same awe I used to feel before. In not too distant a past, on the occasions of betrothal my eyes used to well up thinking of the future the young lad and the young lass would create for themselves. I used to imagine them having children and growing old together. The fresh young faces they were sprouting would wilt and become crumpled versions of what they were. I used to conjure the image of the young couple becoming old and looking back at the wedding pictures of which I was a part of and talk of the old times and ways.

These days, I cannot engage in wishful thinking knowing that there is a good chance that will not happen, not with their being by each other's side anyway. I feel frustrated that my own fairytale of them is so ruthlessly broken and I am denied the free hand to feel the tender feelings towards them. When people say life has become mechanical, I support that sentiment in only one realm—it is in the case of relationships. Our relationships have become more transactional and I bemoan that. Nothing is ever done for its own sake. There is a profit motive behind every action. On logical grounds, there is nothing to fault in that line of thinking but I oppose it vehemently purely on the grounds of my own romantic feelings towards life. I know it is no argument at all, but I also know I am utterly helpless to prove my point any other way.

I find myself taking trips down the memory lane often. I guess when you have a lot of free time in your hands, you are tempted to look back at the life it was. I think of the time when you and I were inseparable. How I constantly used to be in your house and your mother would pamper me as though I was her own. I was fondly recalling the time when a monkey had entered your home in the middle of the day. I was hanging around in your place and we both must have been what, five years old? Your big sister who was also there with her newborn baby took us to a room and sheltered us from the monkey's unknown and unpredictable intentions. It was such a tender age and we couldn't have possibly thought of all that was to come later. When we grew up, there was no big sister to protect us from life's unfathomable intentions, however. I must acknowledge that I have been relatively lucky with regard to life's caprices. Life never threw knock-out punches at me. Not yet, I must add quickly because you cannot ever say it's done until it's fully done. I cannot help but think that you probably had had it a bit more rough. You were triumphant on one front—money wise but I feel in my bones that you were not blessed with the domestic bliss for long. I do not for sure know how afflicted you were but I think being in an unstable state in your personal domain will not be exactly soothing. Anyway, the time has come for you to make one more decision in life—to return to India. There are no secrets between us. That is to say, don't for a moment think you have to maintain an image of strength before me. That is not necessary. I will treat you as my own. Give yourself a chance to make your last days

be as peaceful as they can be. Allow me to be
a participant in the final act of yours.

Love,
Saroja

Chapter X. The Last Letter

Dear Saroja,

As the nurse read the letter you had so beautifully penned, tears had started rolling down her cheeks. I am in an assisted living facility somewhere in Pennsylvania. I have lost physical strength, but otherwise I guess I am quite OK. I am writing the letter on my own because I thought it is only proper that I write the last words and the last letter to you before I lose the ability to do pretty much anything. I have a lot to say and a lot to share, yet I feel what I might say is redundant. What I would really want to say and feel in the heart of my hearts is ineffable too. At least I do not possess the gift of words and the clarity of mind to put them to words. You may think I must be sad living in a remote land all alone. In a sense I am. That is undeniable. For the life that I had built, that was the inevitable denouement. At another level, I am only stoic. I had the life I had, for better or worse. What in the end I feel was important was that I had to experience it, which I did. It is too late in the game for me to complain about what wasn't or have regrets about what I cannot go back and change. I have come to a state of acceptance.

As you can imagine, for someone who does not have much to do, I have given it a lot of thought. I have come to the conclusion that people around me are my people, strangers, or kith and kin, alike. The attendants in the center and my fellow oldies are my family. When I think of the situation from that angle, I come to think what a remarkable life I have had. It was an improbable journey from the ghettos of Mumbai (sorry, but that is what I think you and I lived in) to a posh senior home in Pennsylvania.

I have to fill you in on the details about what happened after I had had a car crash that I had told you about in my previous letter to you. My memory is intact. I remember in vivid details not only what had happened in the many decades of my life but also what I had written to you. I recovered soon after that communication. I got back to a new job and to an old life. I didn't philander after that point. I came to think of women as human beings who had intellect, emotions, feelings, and above all, hearts that are kinder, gentler, nobler than that of men. At any rate, they had better hearts than mine at least. I developed genuine relationships with them. I use the plural form to denote women here because I had a series of relationships. I didn't blow up any one of them. I would have been happy sticking to the first person I was seeing for the rest of my life. Legitimate reasons such as estrangement of thoughts, uprooting of their or my life etc made us sever ties in all cases. Life was not turbulent anymore. I was never a saint in my heart. So I cannot tell you that I engaged in much community service or philanthropy or anything of the kind. But, I was a respectable man in life from that point. I am thrilled to be able to write that to you now because it matters to me more than anything else when I am clearly in the twilight of my life. Something else also changed which I think was more crucial to the stability of my mind and life. It was—faith. Life as we know it is capricious. Most of the time we cannot make sense of it. The logical mind, however, does not come to accept the capriciousness life has to throw at you without resistance. There is another intellectual problem associated with the ups and downs of life. It is the question of, "why bother about anything at all?" If the results do not necessarily follow your actions, then what is the point of your good actions? Those that cannot believe in God grapple with this question all their lives. With any amount of effort, you cannot arrive at a satisfactory solution to the conundrum that I just posited. Faith is a neat alternative. If you believe there is God who bestows the happiness and the sadness that visit you, then you suddenly are off the hook. It simply releases the pressure off of you to perform. The intellectual theory I propounded to you is fine as an elegant answer to the unpredictability of our beings. An atheist, a theist, and everyone in between would accept the two paths as two possible alternative explanations to the theory of life. Even while knowing it, you cannot just one day declare to embrace one or the other. Your mind will not embrace faith only because it is a concept that is comforting. Faith ought to take roots deeper and has to descend on you rather than you actively go seek it. That is what happened to me—on a Monday when I was driving back from work, faith came to me. It changed everything.

The freeways (highways) are free-for-all highways to hell. When you are driving at 100 miles an hour and are surrounded by hundreds of other cars in all directions, it indeed is a miracle that you reach home with your limbs intact. The speed machines, as I like to call the cars, are a persistent threat to one's life. The irony is, you cannot do away with them. On the

Monday evening that I am alluding to, I witnessed a horrible pile-up. Not only did I witness a horrible pile-up but I was a part of it. I was driving at such a high speed and the shock of it was so great that I do not know how the crash started. But what I remember is, the car in front of me suddenly went off course and hit the wall on the side of the road. I was still in my lane. Soon I realized that there was a mangled truck right in front of me—that is why the car before me must have veered off course. So, I veered too. That's all I remember. I was just numb from shock and I had come to a halt after spinning around in the car for what felt like an eternity. Later I learned that my car had traveled some distance on its side too before straightening itself. When the police came and knocked on the door, I think I must have awoken. The paramedics pulled me out. Gradually I was coming back to my senses. Maybe an hour later when I was lying on a hospital bed and a doctor was examining me, I came to full senses. The medical tests revealed that I was unhurt. The giddiness I had felt was a result of the shock and the physical gyration I had endured during the accident. I was home by 10 PM that night. When I lay down in my bed I had an awakening. I could very well have been one of the five dead drivers that day. But, for no fantastic effort on my part, I had escaped without even a cut. Why? I had no idea. The experience jolted me out of my staid living. I became alive to life. I knew I couldn't take life for granted. I mean it in a literal sense. I was spared that day. I didn't know if it was by design or by accident, and didn't know if my summons were to come the day after, a month after, a year after, or several decades after. I became alert to the possibility of death lurking around in the corner all the time. The incident didn't make me an ardent believer in God overnight. But, it nudged me to explore more—to learn what the great philosophers and theologians of our times and the times of yore had to say on the subject. I devoured the extensive treatises on the philosophy of life and death with a research interest. I dispassionately assessed if there was logical consistency and possible truth to the pronouncements. Truth, that was consistent with my own experiences, my own intellectual understanding. Much like your own spiritual awakening you describe in your letter before the last, I had my own. I found their thoughts and theories to gel well with reality. Then I thought it is possible that there is God and there is a design to the universe. I considered it to be one of the most probable explanations of our existence. But then, I couldn't find any other viable explanation. The deeper you dug on any question, the only logical conclusion you can reach is, there is a God who runs the show. Slowly, the feeling of His presence permeated my daily affairs. I could see Him everywhere. I could sense his benevolent disposition in the garbage truck driver for he was engaging in a noble act of keeping our communities clean at His behest. I could see Him in the sales girl assisting me with a smile as I went about the business of buying a shirt that fitted me. I could see Him in my girlfriend when she was showering me with unconditional love. Once you feel God, there is no end to where you can see Him for He is present everywhere. So, I am not sad, I am not bitter at this late stage in my life. I didn't win freedoms for any country the kinds of which Great Gandhi did. I didn't bring solace to the suffering masses like Mother Teresa did. Yet, I lived a life that I was supposed to have. And, what's gratifying is, I am not dying not knowing Him. I am dying knowing He is my father. That is good enough for me.

The physical pain ebbs and flows. I have to say with passing time it is only going up. I had dreamed of living an independent life till I died.

What made it impossible was my inability to drive. The vision had blurred. Despite the cataract surgeries in both eyes, the eyes couldn't see as clearly as before. When the driver's license was due to be renewed and I went to the DMV (Department of Motor Vehicles) office to renew my license, I failed the eye test miserably. There was no way they were going to grant me a license to drive. There was barely a month left on the license. I had to hurriedly sell off the car and look for a retirement home. For everything you have to drive here—at least in the rural part of Pennsylvania where I have lived. For groceries, for a doctor's check-up, and for everything. If I didn't drive, I couldn't visit my Church and couldn't see my friends either. I had taken to going to a Church regularly. Faith coming from any religious denomination is not an issue if you feel the universality and oneness of Him. That is what forced my hand. I have my own apartment in the facility. It is modeled after a hotel suite. It has a bedroom, a small kitchen, and a bathroom. It is quite comfortable. I can socialize with fellow retirees as much or as little as I want. I mostly keep to myself. The things they talk about do not interest me. They talk of American football, and country music hundred percent of the time. As it happens, I do not have a great interest in either of those subjects. What interests me are books, philosophy, and politics. So, I am without intellectual company. I make up for it by phoning my old buddies. I wish I could write to you often, talk to you often. I might. We haven't spoken to each other in ages. Although we have been in touch, we are essentially strangers now I think. But, heck, why don't we give it a try? Thanks for your heartfelt letter and the kindest invitation to move back to India. Unfortunately, I can't. America is my home now. I will be a fish out of water if I were to uproot myself at this stage of my life. I think I will feel worse. The thought of moving back to India hadn't crossed my mind in the last thirty years. I had made America my home. I had embraced its citizenship. I vote in its elections. I feel invested in its future. The balance of belonging had tipped sometime ago: America is more of my land than India is.

I am sorry for your terrible loss. You have lost the love of your life. I do not know what words might bring you comfort for no words can. But know this—you were lucky. I tell it to you because I know how hard it is to find a compatible partner and how rare and lucky it is to spend a lifetime with them. You were lucky on both counts. I have always wished well for you both. In a sense, I was living a vicarious life in you—you were everything that I was not. You were devoted to your family, you had a firm sense of what was right and what was wrong. You were the ideal that I could never be. You wished to stay back in India despite your being more brilliant than me. You could have been in any part of the world today. You chose to be home. That I think is a far more blissful place than a palatial home one could build elsewhere. I am proud of you and proud of your choices. I have always had a possessive zeal to see you be in the right. I wanted you to be perfect. The slightest of deviations from perfection would make me uncomfortable because with it my dream of you would suffer a crack. You kept my stuff of the dreams intact. Through to the end, you showed how to lead an honorable life, how to maintain grace in the face of adversity, how to navigate the airplane of life through turbulent weather and to land it safely. Land safely, you did. Do you know what ails me the most to this day? Not attending my mother's funeral. I was living a high flying life then. When the news came, I was in the middle of a business trip. Plus, my girlfriend was with me. I was in Los

Angeles. We had made plans to make a trip up to Las Vegas. She was my prize catch—my girlfriend was. Truth be told, it was the burning desire to be ensconced in the hot body of hers that kept me from going to India. I made up all sorts of inane excuses to my brother—how it was a high profile customer that I was desperately trying to retain for my company etc. It's a regret I will carry to the end. The idiom "As you sow so shall you reap" is packed with truth. If I couldn't be at my own mother's bedside while she was dying, what right do I have to expect someone else to be at my bedside during my own end? I don't. I have reconciled myself to that fact. I try to keep the thought of having been bereft of a family out of my mind. It has a way of sneaking back in. I have paid for the rest of my life in this center by making a generous endowment to its coffers. I still have a couple of million dollars left in my bank account. You know it can't buy me goodwill or people though.

I admired you when we were growing up. We were close, very close. Nobody understood me as you did and I dare say, nobody understood you as I did too. I knew from the beginning where your heart lay—your family and your country. I decided early on that I will not propose to you because that would have stood in the way of my scheme of flying away. Flying away from the strait-jacket my parents had imposed around me was the goal that obsessed me day in and day out. Their old ways of conducting business, for example to not install a modern geyser to heat the bath water and instead use a gas stove still, I thought were anachronistic with the modernity that already had swept Mumbai. And, I was right. So as you can imagine when I had got the chance to build a new life in the promised land of America I had to take it. In a hypothetical reality if I had stayed back, I think I would have died a bitter man. I am glad I took the chance. I wish I could tell you that if I had proposed to you in the youth, the course of life would have been more wonderful for us both. I do not think so. Your and my goals in life were quite different. It would be foolhardy to clip our ambitions to retrofit to a life we cannot wholeheartedly embrace. I wish for a time when we both could see eye to eye on every matter of life or at least on most important decisions of life. In the end I think we both were better off for the lives we came to live. I cannot tell you how much I miss you. You have remained in my memory every single day of my life. Your beautiful face flashes across me, the new song you had hummed on the way back home after we had watched the new Bollywood movie at midnight rings in my ears as though it is happening now. Your thoughts, your innocent dreams, and your impeccable sense of fairness are ever reverberating in my mind. I wish we could be together. I wish I could lend you a shoulder to cry on. I wish I could blow away the crippling loneliness you feel. I wish I had the warmth of your love for myself.

I never got to meet your daughters. Do they look like you? Do they think like you? I am pretty sure I will get along with them well — if I can get along with you, then I am sure I can get along fairly well with modern women who have got your genes. Do kiss your grandkids for me. Thanks for a lifetime of friendship. Hope to see you on the other side.

Love,
Akash